S0-DTA-809

# Sunday's Child

# SUNDAY'S CHILD

## BY GUDRUN MEBS

□

*Dial Books for Young Readers*
*New York*

Park Orchard Library

First published in the United States 1986 by
Dial Books for Young Readers
2 Park Avenue,
New York, New York 10016

Published simultaneously in Canada by
Fitzhenry & Whiteside Limited, Toronto
First published in English in 1984
This translation © 1984 by Andersen Press Ltd.
First published in German in 1983
as *Sonntagskind* © 1983 by Verlag Saaerländer,
Aarau, Switzerland

Translated by Sarah Gibson

All rights reserved
Design by Nancy R. Leo
Printed in U.S.A.
First Edition
C O B E
2 4 6 8 10 9 7 5 3 1

Library of Congress Cataloging in Publication Data
Mebs, Gudrun. Sunday's child.
Translation of: Sonntagskind.
Summary: Ten-year-old Jenny's new foster mother
doesn't live up to her expectations until Jenny discovers
that there are more important things in life
than lavish gifts and fancy homes.
[1. Foster home care—Fiction.
2. Mothers and daughters—Fiction.] I. Title.
PZ7.M51267Su 1986 [Fic.] 85-20629
ISBN 0-8037-0192-6
ISBN 0-8037-0197-7 (lib. bdg.)

For Stefano

# SUNDAY'S CHILD

## Chapter 1

I am a Sunday's Child. That is, I was born on a Sunday. Supposedly, children born on Sunday are lucky, but I don't think so. Anyway, I hate Sundays more than any other day. It's so boring on Sundays in the Home.

I've lived in the Home for a long time, all my life, in fact, because my parents couldn't keep me when I was a baby. No one's ever told me why, at least, not exactly. Just something about "the circumstances were not right." I don't know what that means. At first I was too little to ask, and later I was scared to. Now I think they just didn't want me.

When I was little, I was always looking for my parents. Whenever we went for a walk or shopping or anything, I always looked at people. Married couples. Or anyone who looked like parents. I was pretty stupid then. And it got boring too, searching and searching for something that didn't exist.

I remember the time I saw two people in a store, a lady and a man, and they looked like they could be my parents. I tore my hand away from Sister Linda's and ran up to the man and the lady and called out, "Daddy, Mommy!" They just stared at me. Sister Linda blushed and grabbed me by the hand again and apologized to the people and then got mad at me. I was ashamed because I had already figured out that the people couldn't possibly be my parents. Not the way they'd looked at me! Nothing like that ever happened again. I was still just a silly kid then.

It's all different now. I haven't looked for my parents for a long time. It's stupid to look for someone you don't even know. They might even be dead. At least Andrea thinks they are.

Andrea shares a room with me. We're lucky because we have a double room. It's got a bunk bed and two desks to do homework on. It's great. Andrea sleeps on the top bunk and I sleep on the bottom. Andrea hardly ever wants to trade. She's only twelve, just two years older than me, but she acts like that gives her a right to everything! I think we should take turns, but I never can win against Andrea.

Andrea's parents are both dead. It's sad, because Andrea knew them, both of them. At least I never knew my parents, so I've never really missed them.

It's actually pretty nice in the Home. The house is kind of old-fashioned and it has a garden all around it. It used to be a mansion, but now it's used as an orphanage, and it's full of orphans. Secretly we call it the Poop Hole, but only secretly, because if Sister Frances ever heard us call it that, she'd really get mad. Sister Frances is the oldest of the sisters, and she's responsible for all of us. Sister Linda is a lot younger, and she's responsible for us too, but not as much.

With so many kids living together things can get pretty wild. Sometimes we just get on each other's nerves. I'm sure brothers and sisters get on each other's nerves too. Even though at the Home we live together like brothers and sisters, at least we don't have to see each other all day long. We all go to different grades in school. I'm the only one in my grade. I mean, there are lots of other kids, but they aren't from the Home. They come from their own homes like regular kids.

I get along well with kids—with the kids in my class and with the ones in the Home too. Except on

Sundays! Most of them get to go out on Sundays. And the ones that don't are in a bad mood because they can't.

Here's how it works: Almost all of us at the Home have Sunday Foster Parents. These are parents who want to take care of a child on Sundays, and so they come to the Home and pick one. Then that child is called a Sunday Foster Child and is allowed to go out with them every Sunday, and longer at Christmas and Easter. It's really great! You get picked up and then brought back again at night, usually in a car. Most of the Sunday Foster Parents have cars. They're the best kind of parents because they always take you on fantastic trips. To the zoo, or the park, or somewhere. After that you go and eat ice cream, and in the winter you have dinner in a restaurant and get presents. All the kids at the Home think Sundays are the best. And when they come back, they talk about their Sundays for hours. I get sick and tired of hearing it all. I don't believe most of it. Such huge amounts of ice cream . . . loads of cookies . . . and watching television *all* day long . . . and getting new felt pens.

Last Sunday Andrea got a new blouse. Just like that. I would like a new blouse too, and I'd like to go and eat ice cream with some Sunday Foster Parents. But no one has ever picked me; I can't figure out why.

Last year a fat man, and a woman with lots of beautiful little curls all over her head, came who wanted a Sunday Foster Child. So Sister Frances called me in, but I had just gotten a terrible cold and my face looked all red and swollen. When they saw me, they stepped back, and the lady put her handkerchief up to her nose. Nothing more ever happened, so I just went on spending Sundays alone in the Home—the older kids didn't play with me and I didn't play with the little kids. I usually just waited around or sometimes I'd go out for a walk in the garden. Then when the others came back at night and started to brag, I was always jealous.

But now I don't have to be jealous anymore. Because now I've got Sunday Foster Parents too! I mean, they're not parents, it's just a lady, but still!

Yesterday, on Sunday afternoon, Sister Frances sent this stupid kid named Donny to get me. Donny is much littler than me. I never play with him. He always drools when he talks and he stutters too. He's a little crazy, if you ask me. He's got hair like a haystack, all stiff and yellow, and he never knocks before he comes into your room.

When I finally got Donny to say that Sister Frances

7

wanted to see me, I was worried. Usually when she calls you, it means something bad.

But this time it wasn't anything bad—far from it! Sister Frances patted my head very gently, something she hardly ever does, and then, because she was right up close to me, she buttoned up my sweater and said, "So, Jenny—now you're going to be a Foster Child too—aren't you pleased?"

At first I didn't understand. I felt so hot with my sweater buttoned up, and Sister Frances is always so direct, she blurted it out too fast for me to follow.

I think I must have looked pretty stupid. She said it again. "Aren't you pleased?" I nodded because she seemed to expect me to. Then it slowly began to sink in. A Foster Child—that meant Sunday Foster Parents! And if Sister Frances was telling *me* about it, that meant *my* Sunday Foster Parents!

I blushed and started to stutter, just like that stupid Donny. "For me? Sunday Foster Parents for me?"

But then Sister Frances shook her head and said, "No, it's not parents. It's a very nice lady, and she has picked you."

Now, *that* I couldn't understand. Picked me? How could she have picked me if she hadn't ever seen me? They always inspect you before picking you to be a Sunday Foster Child. I was sure nobody had picked me or I would have noticed it.

Then Sister Frances began to explain. She told me that a lady had come who wanted a Sunday Foster Child very much, and that she didn't care if it was a boy or a girl. The lady also didn't care what age and she didn't care what the child looked like. She would take any child that Sister Frances suggested. "So then I thought of you!" said Sister Frances and buttoned up the top button of my sweater.

The first thing I thought was, Well, at least she didn't suggest that stupid Donny. He doesn't have Sunday Foster Parents either, but in his case that isn't really surprising.

Then I thought, Actually, I would rather have two parents, a Sunday Daddy and a Sunday Mommy. But I decided not to go on with this thought. Maybe it was a good thing that the lady hadn't seen me. After all, no one had wanted me before. But now she had to have me because Sister Frances had arranged it.

And then I began to be happy. When I'm happy, I get all tingly in my stomach, and I was tingly then . . . right there in Sister Frances's room. I didn't let it show, though. I just curtsied and said, "Thank you very much," and went out of the door really fast.

"You'll be picked up next Sunday," Sister Frances called after me, "I'll expect you to . . ." But I didn't hear the rest; I had already run up the stairs and into my room. I sat there on my bed and held Cuddly-Bunny on my lap. I unbuttoned my sweater too. I felt very hot, and not just because of the sweater.

I was going to be picked up next Sunday! Like all the other children, just like them! By a Sunday Mommy! It didn't matter that she wasn't my real mother. The most important thing was that somebody wanted me and was going to pick me up. A Sunday Mommy just for me! I said the words quietly out loud, "Sunday Mommy!" and pressed Cuddly-Bunny against my cheek as I said them.

Cuddly-Bunny is my best friend and always has been. I've almost sucked his ears off and he just listens and listens. He's always with me, except for in school. Cuddly-Bunny has blue-and-white checked pants and beautiful dark brown eyes—very big and very wise. I would love to have eyes like his, but mine are a mixture of green, gray, and blue. And there's nothing I can do about that.

Supposedly, a nurse in the hospital gave me Cuddly-Bunny when I was born. They tell me I would never go to sleep unless I had Cuddly-Bunny next to me on my pillow. That still hasn't changed.

For a long time I kept repeating, "Sunday Mommy, Sunday Mommy!" out loud to Cuddly-Bunny, and Cuddly-Bunny looked at me patiently with his brown button eyes, and I suddenly realized I had forgotten to ask what my Sunday Mommy's name was. Sister Frances could at least have told me that. Probably she forgot . . . but I didn't dare go down again now and knock on the door to ask her. I'd find out on Sunday, anyway.

I snuggled with Cuddly-Bunny under my blankets and sucked on his ears a little and murmured, "Sunday Mommy, Sunday Mommy!" It sounded nice! And then I started to imagine all the things I'd do with my Sunday Mommy. First, I would like to go to the zoo and eat lots of ice cream, raspberry ice cream, banana ice cream, green ice cream, chocolate ice cream . . . but maybe there wouldn't be any ice cream because it was still pretty cold. Oh, well, I'd have cake then, lots and lots. Especially chocolate cake with whipped cream on top. Then we'd go see the monkeys and feed them peanuts. And then we'd go see the snakes, because I think snakes are beautiful. They're so incredibly long and they can curl up and swallow mice whole. And then we'd go for a ride in the park in her car. Would she have a car? Of course she would, nearly everyone had a car—

hers would be special. Then we'd go for a walk, and then we'd have a picnic or go to a restaurant, and I would eat hot dogs. At least three of them, and no salad. And then we'd drive to her apartment. Where would she live? She'd probably have a big apartment, with lots of rooms, all to herself. There'd be a huge garden in front with a swimming pool, and in the apartment she would have a real fireplace with a bearskin rug. I saw that once on television and I really liked it. We would sit on the bearskin rug and make ourselves comfortable, and then we'd eat something. Potato chips. I love potato chips. We never get them here, only at Christmastime. . . .

Oh, yes, we'd do all that, and then at night she would bring me back to the Home, maybe with a real chauffeur wearing a uniform and a cap. I'd get out of the car, and he would open the door for me, and all the children in the Home would stare and be jealous and then . . . Then I must have fallen asleep. It was already dark outside.

Something made a noise and I woke up. Andrea! She rushed into the room, dumped her coat and hat on my bed, and yelled, "Sleepyhead! Sleepyhead! Are you taking a nap, Jenny? Wake up! You'll never guess what I did today!"

Of course I'd never guess, and I could care less,

anyway. But that made no difference to Andrea. She began telling me something about a fantastic long walk in the park and an incredible lunch. There was a casserole followed by rice pudding, and then everyone played Monopoly for hours and hours. It had been the best Sunday ever.

How boring can you get? Casserole, rice pudding! It was pitiful. But Andrea didn't know anything yet about my new Sunday Mommy, so I got up to tell her. I left Cuddly-Bunny in the bed; there was no reason for Andrea to see him. She always makes fun of him, anyway. I stood in front of Andrea and said just one thing. Just this: "Well? So what?"

Andrea shut her mouth and stared at me. "So what?" I repeated, and then I said, "I've got a Sunday Mommy, and she's going to do much nicer things with me than your silly old Sunday Parents do with you!"

"What do you have?" Andrea was still staring.

"A Sunday Mommy, are you deaf?" I said, and sat down on my bed. Then Andrea started asking me a million questions. Since when, and why, and how, and why only a Mommy, why not parents, and what was her name, and where did she live?

I actually didn't have much to tell, since I didn't know anything myself yet. But for once I wanted

Andrea to be jealous of me. I told her everything I'd imagined about the apartment and more. There were golden armchairs and a golden sofa, covered in silk, and glass tables with silver feet, and on the tables stood enormous boxes of candy and enormous bowls of potato chips, and there was a fireplace with a real fire burning, and in front of the fireplace lay a polar bearskin with a real head. It looked alive, and in its mouth it had—it had—a golden apple!

Andrea sat back and listened, with her mouth open. Up to the part about the golden apple. Then she shot forward and said, "Golden apple, my foot! There's no such thing!"

"There is in my Sunday Mommy's apartment!" I protested, but it didn't sound convincing. Maybe the golden apple in the polar bear's mouth had been too much!

Andrea tapped me on the forehead and whispered mockingly, "And how do you know all this when you've never been there? Come on, you made it all up!"

First I said nothing, then I admitted it. What choice did I have? "But," I said, and slid away from Andrea a little, "I bet my Sunday Mommy's apartment really does look a little like that."

Andrea grinned. "Yeah, and what does she look

like, your Sunday Mommy?" She said "Sunday Mommy" as if she didn't believe in her, either.

But she really did exist, Sister Frances said so, and Sister Frances never made things up. Never! What *did* my Sunday Mommy look like? I closed my eyes and pictured her. "She's tall and very thin, and she wears a fur coat, a really expensive, soft one, and she has long red curly hair and . . . yellow eyes!"

"Yellow eyes?" Andrea interrupted rudely. "Yellow eyes? No one has yellow eyes, you're lying!" She pinched my arm. That's a really annoying habit of hers.

But today I just pinched her back and said quickly, "Okay, she doesn't have yellow eyes, she has blue ones, if you must know, as blue as forget-me-nots."

"You're just a liar!" said Andrea in a slow, nasty way.

I am not! I don't lie, I just made it up. Making things up isn't lying! I didn't say anything. I just turned away and buried my head in my pillow.

Right away Andrea pulled me up and I thought, Uh-oh. She's going to pinch me again. But instead Andrea grinned at me, a nice, ordinary grin, and said, "Oh, come on, don't get so worked up, you little liar! Tell me more about the amazing apartment, and the amazing lady, and maybe she's got an

Park Orchard Library

amazing dog, and everything about her is amazing!"

I just had to laugh. That's typical of Andrea! One minute she's horrible, the next really nice.

So I started to tell her again, and Andrea talked too. We each described the apartment, the colors, and the furniture, even the bowls of food and candy on the tables.

But when I said there was a fireplace made of marble and a fantastic coal fire burning in it, Andrea began to laugh. "Coal!" she screeched. "You don't have coal fires in a fireplace! Wood, you idiot! It's got to be wood!"

Oh, all right, all right, wood, then! I could care less, and anyhow, how was I supposed to know? I'd never seen a fireplace in real life—only on television and in photographs. But I could imagine it anyway: A fire was burning and it was so cozy and warm, and in front of it lay a polar bearskin. Then we started fighting about that too. Andrea wanted a giraffe skin, but I thought it was a stupid idea. "Giraffe skin! Its neck would be much too long. It wouldn't fit into the room!"

While we were still arguing about it, the bell rang and we had to wash our hands and go down to Sunday supper. "I'm still going to have a giraffe skin!" Andrea said as she ran out the door.

"And I'm going to have a polar bearskin!" I shouted after her. "Whose apartment is it, anyway?"

After supper we were allowed to do what we wanted for a while, and then it was snip, snap, and into bed, as Sister Linda would say. Then she would come and say good night, and sometimes, if we were lucky, she would read to us for a while. But that didn't happen often. Sister Linda is nice, but "thoroughly overworked," as she keeps telling us. Tonight I didn't mind not getting a story. I just wanted to get into bed quickly and cuddle up with Cuddly-Bunny and think about things for a while—about the fantastic apartment and about my Sunday Mommy. . . .

I knew I wouldn't go to sleep. So much had happened. My stomach was tingling and tingling. If only it were Sunday already! Six more days to go—Monday, Tuesday, Wednesday, Thursday, Friday, Saturday. That'd take forever. I was sure I couldn't wait. What would I wear? I'd like to wear something nice, something new. But we almost never get anything new in this place. Just hand-me-downs from the older kids. I would love to have one of those glittery pullover sweaters and a new pair of jeans for once, jeans that fit and didn't always bag around the waist and have to be rolled up.

Maybe my Sunday Mommy would give me something new if I asked nicely. But it would probably be pushing it to ask for a glittery sweater and a new pair of jeans the first time I meet her. Maybe I could ask at Christmas. I was sure my Mommy would have lots of money. She would be so rich, she could buy anything she wanted. In one of the stories Sister Linda read us once it said, "And they lived like kings and queens." I thought my Sunday Mommy would live like that.

At last I felt like I really was a Sunday's Child. Because from now on, Sunday was going to be my lucky day!

# Chapter 2

It was Sunday—the day I was going to be picked up!

I woke up early, much earlier than usual, feeling really happy, and I rushed to the bathroom. There wasn't anybody else there, so I washed for a long time, and I brushed my hair for ages, even though it didn't do any good. My hair's really thin, and it hangs down straight like string. Anyway, that's what Andrea says. She says lots of awful things, but unfortunately she's right about my hair. At least my cheeks looked pink from the cold water, I thought, and I slipped quickly back to our room. Andrea was still asleep up in the top bunk, and for once I was glad she slept on the top, so she couldn't see that I had secretly taken her new blouse. I didn't want to keep it forever, just for today. Andrea would never lend me something like that. Only if I begged and begged her, and I hate begging.

The blouse was big on me because Andrea is fatter than I am, but at least it was new. I put my sweater on over it so that Andrea wouldn't notice it at breakfast. Otherwise there'd be a big fight.

Actually, I wasn't hungry at all. My stomach felt glued up. We always had rolls for breakfast on Sundays—and there were cornflakes too. But that didn't matter if you didn't feel hungry.

I had to go to breakfast, though, because Sister Linda came to get me. They're very strict about breakfast at the Home. They tell us it's good to put something inside you in the morning, and no arguing is allowed. So I passed my roll and my cornflakes to Andrea, then I drank my hot chocolate quickly and left.

Sister Frances caught me outside, and I thought, Now she's going to yell at me because we're not actually allowed to leave the table early. But she didn't yell at me; she pulled me over, tugged at my sweater, and smoothed down my hair. There was no need to smooth down my hair, it's smooth anyway. Then she said, "Make sure you behave yourself today. Mind your manners and be polite, just as you've been taught. Don't disgrace us now, will you?"

I said yes to all of it. What else could I say? And then she asked me whether I had a clean handkerchief, and of course I didn't, so she gave me hers. Sometimes Sister Frances is really nice. Her handkerchieves are very fancy—they're white and have little red flowers embroidered in the corners. I like them. But then, of course, she had to warn me not to lose it. That's typical of her. Right after she's been nice, she gets all bossy again.

I thanked her for the handkerchief because she expected it, and then I sat down in the hallway and began to wait.

And there I was, still sitting! The others had all left long ago. That was some performance! I'd never been part of it before, because on Sundays I always used to hide so that I wouldn't see all the others being picked up. But today I saw everything. It seemed as if everyone arrived at the same time! *Bang, crash,* the door kept opening and parents kept coming in, and children came down the stairs and looked for their jackets, and the parents all gave their children kisses, and everyone was talking and calling and shouting. And in the middle of all this commotion stood Sister Frances, giving advice, and it was like recess in the playground at school.

Then suddenly everyone was gone. The hall was

quiet and empty. There was just Donny hanging around, making snotty sniffing noises and drooling. No one had come for him. I wouldn't either, he's so stupid. Not like me, I was going to be picked up!

Only, where could she be, this Sunday Mommy? Suppose I wasn't going to be picked up after all? Suppose she'd forgotten? Or maybe she'd decided she didn't want to have a child? But then Sister Frances would have told me. She wouldn't have forgotten. Sister Frances isn't like that. She's very conscientious; in fact, she says so herself and expects all of us to be too.

But maybe my Sunday Mommy had looked through the glass door secretly and seen me while I was sitting there left behind all by myself, and had realized I must be her Sunday's Child, and she was horrified and said to herself, "Yuck, I don't want her!" Or maybe, even worse, she saw Donny because he was still hanging around, and because my Sunday Mommy didn't know whether she was supposed to be getting a boy or a girl, she thought Donny must be the one and quickly left because he looks so awful, much worse than me.

But I hadn't seen anyone look through the door. I was sure of that. I'd been staring at the door all the time, at least since a quarter to nine. I would have seen anyone who went away.

Maybe she was sick and couldn't come. But then she would have sent someone else or called, and the phone hasn't rung. I would have heard it because it's right in the hall. Maybe she was so sick that she had to be rushed to the hospital and didn't have time to call. Then she'd be lying in a hospital bed feeling sorry for me.

That really was silly. She didn't even know me yet. But then, why hadn't she come? I just couldn't imagine why, and suddenly my stomach felt really hollow, probably because I hadn't had any breakfast. Then a tear trickled down my cheek. I wiped the stupid tear away quickly, before Donny saw. I shouted a little at him and told him not to stare at me. Then I pretended I had a cold and blew my nose in the handkerchief Sister Frances had given me. I felt badly about that. It was so pretty, and I had wanted to use it for the first time at my Sunday Mommy's house.

I wished I had Cuddly-Bunny with me. He would understand; I wouldn't have to pretend I had a cold. In fact, I could go and cuddle with him now, he was upstairs on my bed. My Sunday Mommy was definitely not going to come. Maybe I'd just dreamed the whole thing and it was just an ordinary Sunday like all the others. I stood up and was about to go when there was Sister Linda coming down the stairs. She saw me and asked in astonishment, "What, hasn't Miss Fielder come yet?"

I stood where I was and just stared blankly at Sister Linda. And then I figured it out. Miss Fielder! That must be my Sunday Mommy! So that was her name. Miss Fielder!

But she hadn't come. So I shook my head, and as I shook my head I started to cry again, and Sister Linda came all the way downstairs and said, "Now, now!" and wiped my eyes with a tissue. "There!" she said. "We'll just go and tele—" She didn't have time to say "phone," because at that moment the glass door flew open and someone rushed inside in such a hurry that she almost ran into Sister Linda and me.

And the someone was out of breath, and the someone was a woman, and she said in a breathless voice, as if she had run a long way, "Please, where can I find Sister Frances? I'm late, and I want to pick up my child."

"Well," said Sister Linda, pointing to the clock, "you certainly are late. Sister Frances has gone upstairs"—she pointed to the stairs—"and the child is here. Her name is Jenny," she said. And I just stood there with Sister Frances's tissue over my nose. I'm sure my eyes were swollen and I must have looked awful! And there in front of me stood my Sunday Mommy. Miss Fielder! First I thought there must be some mistake, this couldn't be her. She didn't look like a woman, but like a boy. She was wearing a rubber hat and raincoat. No sign of a fur anywhere!

But her voice did sound like a woman's voice, so she must be one. But she was so small, only a little taller than me. For a grown-up she was really tiny! I couldn't see much of her face because her rubber hat was pulled down almost to her nose and she was wearing glasses, really stupid ones with round lenses. She didn't look at all like the Sunday Mommy Andrea and I had imagined. I could forget all that junk about the fireplace and the chauffeur and the bearskin. She didn't even have red hair. She didn't say anything either, she just stood there with her hands in her pockets, blinking at me through her glasses.

So this was my Sunday Mommy!

I knew I should say, "Good morning, Sunday Mommy," or at least, "Good morning, Miss Fielder, thank you very much for taking me out," or some-

thing like that. But I couldn't, I just couldn't—
something seemed to be stuck in my throat.

Then someone wriggled between Sister Linda and
me and stepped on my foot. It was that stupid little
Donny, being nosy as usual. He always has to be
there. "Ouch!" I cried, dropping the tissue, and I
rubbed my foot and began to sob.

Well, my foot didn't really hurt that much, but
it helped to cry. Donny stared stupidly at me,
Sister Linda put an arm around my shoulders, and
Miss Fielder bent down and ruffled Donny's hair.
Just once, but I saw it. No, it wasn't fair. She'd
touched the wrong person! *I'm* her Sunday Child, I
thought.

Through my sobbing I heard Sister Linda say,
"Why don't we all go and have some cocoa?" She
held Donny's hand and disappeared in the direction
of the kitchen with him, leaving me all alone with
the strange lady. I would have liked to have run
after Sister Linda, but I couldn't. So I stood where
I was and sniffed, because my nose really was running now.

Then Miss Fielder bent down and picked up the
handkerchief and held it out to me and said, "There,
there, Jenny." And her voice sounded as if she were
laughing secretly. I had to admit her voice sounded

nice. I blew my nose and she watched me. I blew my nose for a long time. Miss Fielder just stood and waited and looked at me while I blew my nose. Then she said, "Would you like some cocoa?"

I didn't want any. What I really wanted to do was go to bed with Cuddly-Bunny and pull the covers over my head. But that was out, that was for sure! I shook my head, I still couldn't say anything, and then Sister Linda came back, this time without Donny, and she bent down and said softly, "You don't have to go. You can stay here and play with Donny." Play with Donny! That's all I needed! No, I'd much rather go with the strange lady.

"I'd rather go," I said, and so we went. My new Sunday Mommy and me.

But we didn't just go, we ran. All the way to the subway. "We'll just catch it if we hurry!" said Miss Fielder and started off at a spurt. And there was nothing for me to do but run with her. I didn't even wonder why we weren't going in a car. I'd figured out by then that she didn't have a car or a chauffeur. I'd known ever since I saw her that everything would be very, very different from what Andrea and I had imagined.

Miss Fielder lived in a long street with old gray houses. There wasn't a garden in sight, not even a little narrow one like there sometimes is in front of houses. The house that Miss Fielder lived in was gray too and pretty rundown.

We had to climb up lots of stairs to get to her apartment. There wasn't even an elevator. When Miss Fielder nudged me through the door, the first thing I noticed was that it stunk of cigarette smoke. Yuck! We were hardly inside before Miss Fielder lit up a cigarette, and then she showed me the apartment. It was a funny place. Very empty. There was almost no furniture in it, no real furniture, I mean.

First she showed me the kitchen. There was an oven, but only a little one, and the sink was just a tiny basin, and the dishes weren't put away neatly in cabinets but stacked any which way on a shelf. Nothing was sparkling white like in the Home. In fact, it all looked pretty dirty. In the middle of the kitchen stood a huge long table, but it was just a long wide plank on wooden sawhorses like in a carpenter's workshop. I'd seen one in a book once.

And the table itself! Talk about a mess! Piles of paper were lying all over the place and there was a typewriter and pencils and notebooks and an eraser, and everything was stacked on top of each other.

I must have looked amazed because Miss Fielder quickly picked up the papers and pencils and smiled and said, "You must excuse me. You see, this is where I work. I was doing some work before I came to get you."

Doing some work? On Sunday? I didn't know anybody who had to work on Sundays. The other children's Sunday Parents certainly didn't. I'm sure they didn't work at home, either; they worked in an office or somewhere. And I just couldn't imagine what kind of work all this mess on the table was supposed to be! For a moment I thought that maybe I was about to be sent back to the Home, because she had work to do and I would disturb her. But I really didn't want to go back to the Home; there was only that stupid Donny there and I'd see him all week anyway—it might be better to stay here.

I liked the other room better than the kitchen, even though there was almost no furniture in it. The whole floor was covered with a thick white shaggy carpet. It almost looked like a polar bearskin. And there was a big mattress covered with another white rug with tassels. White cushions were scattered around, and the windows had long white curtains, and it all looked really nice. But it was messy there too. Books were spread all over the rug and all over the mattress, and there was a white bookcase stuffed with books too. I wondered if Miss Fielder had read them all. There were so many of them that I was almost sure she hadn't. It made me shudder. I don't like reading, especially not a whole book from beginning to end.

I didn't dare go into the room with my dirty shoes on just in case I got dirt on the carpet. Miss Fielder had taken off her shoes and socks as soon as we came in and was now walking around barefoot.

She noticed I hadn't come into the room because of the carpet, and she said I should just take my shoes off and she'd get me a pair of wooden shoes. What strange things they were! "They're clogs from Holland," she explained, and said they were very comfortable. I didn't think so. They were too big for me and made my legs feel heavy, and they were so clunky, I could only shuffle around slowly. Miss Fielder laughed at me. In fact, she laughed about everything. And all the time she rushed around as if she were really nervous. She had barely looked at me, or me at her. I didn't want to. Anyway, it's rude to stare at people.

She was like a bird, always fluttering around. . . . She called me into the room and said she would fix something to eat and then we could make ourselves comfortable and get to know each other a little. So I shuffled carefully into the room. There was no chair to sit on so I sat on a corner of the mattress. Miss Fielder had zoomed into the workshop-kitchen and was talking to herself. I couldn't really understand what she was saying—it sounded as though she were looking for something.

I looked around the room. What a mess it was! If Sister Frances could have seen it, she would have thrown up her hands in horror, which is what she does when there's anything lying around in our rooms. And here there was a whole pile of things lying around, even dirty socks. And ashtrays everywhere with cigarette butts in them. They stunk. Miss Fielder was still wandering around in the kitchen and suddenly she called loudly, "Jar of honey, now, where have you gone?" I almost laughed out loud. Who ever heard of having a conversation with a jar of honey? As if it would ever answer you!

Then she came back into the room, lugging a big tray that she put down in the middle of the mattress, on top of the books and the cushions. The tray wobbled dangerously, and I quickly grabbed it, otherwise it would have tipped over and everything would have spilled. Miss Fielder plunked herself down next to me and laughed again. There something odd about her. I suddenly realized she wasn't wearing her glasses. She opened her eyes wide,

and her eyes were dark brown just like Cuddly-
Bunny's. Big and brown, Cuddly-Bunny eyes! And
when she laughed, she had lots of tiny little wrinkles
around her eyes. Miss Fielder's hair was like Cuddly-
Bunny's too, very short and dark, standing up all
over, even on top of her head. Cuddly-Bunny's hair
lies nice and flat because I always wet it and comb it
down. Miss Fielder should try it sometime; I might
tell her, but not yet.

She sure wasn't pretty, but I had already decided
she was nice. I think I must have been staring at her
pretty hard, because she suddenly fidgeted around on
the mattress and began to talk a lot. About a lot of
things, quickly one after the other. Her name was
Laura, she said, I must call her Laura, and she lived
by herself, and she had a boyfriend whose name was
Chris, and he lived somewhere else, and they always
spent Sundays together, although they wouldn't anymore, because now I was there, and she hoped I
liked being with her, and she earned her living from
writing, and she wrote children's books, and she had
already had a book published, and she hoped to have
many more, and . . . and . . . and. And all the time she
smeared honey on some pieces of bread, and opened a
couple of cartons of yogurt and stirred them around

with a spoon, and then she jumped up and said she'd forgotten the sugar and ran back to the kitchen. I didn't say anything because she hadn't asked me anything, she had just talked and there was no need to answer.

I wondered how old she was. I couldn't really tell. She certainly didn't look old, because she was so small and thin and kept running around in bare feet and was wearing jeans. But she wasn't that young either because of her wrinkles and because they don't allow young people to take us out of the Home. I was supposed to call her Laura, not Miss Fielder. I had really hoped I could call her Mommy. But she wasn't like a mommy, that was for sure. Mommies look different. Mommies are much quieter and bigger, and mostly they have curly hair and smile kindly and calmly and take care of you.

My Laura-Mommy didn't smile, she laughed, very loudly, and she hadn't gotten mad or cooked anything either. All she'd done so far was to make us a snack, with pieces of bread and honey and yogurt, and tea. She hadn't even cooked.

Then Laura came back into the room with a box of sugar in her hand and poured a whole lot into my mug. I don't like sugar in tea, it makes me feel sick.

What was I going to do now? It was too late to say, "No, thank you very much, I don't take sugar." The sugar was already in, and it wouldn't have been polite not to drink the tea.

First of all I took a slice of bread and honey. I don't really like bread and honey all that much either, and this honey was so gooey that as soon as I had the piece of bread in my hand the honey ran off and dropped onto the nice white carpet. Oh, *no*! I thought.

I hoped she hadn't noticed. She hadn't. Luckily, she wasn't wearing her glasses. I secretly rubbed at the stain, but it wouldn't go away, it just got bigger and browner. I was so scared, I just stuffed the rest of the bread into my mouth all at once. I choked a little on it, and because it wouldn't go down, I took a gulp of tea. With sugar. And suddenly I felt sick. Not that on top of everything else!

But Laura didn't notice a thing. Laura went on talking and fidgeted around on the mattress. I just couldn't pay attention, all I could think of was, I hope she doesn't see the stain. I hope I'm not going to be sick. Sugar in tea always makes me sick, but I really didn't want to be this time, I didn't even know where the bathroom was, and I was feeling hot, and Laura went on talking.

"Writing," I heard her say, and my stomach heaved.

"Concentration," I heard her say, and I could feel the tea rising up in my throat.

"For children," I heard her say, and I pushed hard into my stomach so the tea would stay down.

"Read together," I heard her say, and the tea came up in my throat again.

"Nice Sundays," I heard her say, and then the tea was in my mouth and shot out. All over me and the white rug and the honey stain and the carpet.

Laura stopped talking and opened her eyes wide, and I shut mine tight. Now it was all over. She'd never forgive me. Any minute she'd start yelling at me. I really couldn't help it; it was the tea's fault. It was her fault, actually, because she'd put sugar in my tea, and what I really wanted to do was to cry.

But she didn't start yelling; all she did was leave the room. I heard a splashing, like water coming out of a faucet. Then she was back. She still didn't say anything, she just picked me up and managed to get a lot of yucky vomit on herself, but she wasn't mad. She just shuffled into the bathroom with me and didn't say anything about the messed-up rug or the messed-up carpet. She started to undress me as if I were a baby. She undid my blouse, Andrea's blouse, which was covered with vomit too and stunk. There'd be a big scene about that, but I could have cared less because I felt awful. Really awful.

Laura undressed me till I was completely naked, and I didn't care, because I felt so awful. Then she said, "Okay, Jenny, hop into the tub!" I got in, and the water was nice and hot, and there were bubbles, and it smelled wonderful. And I quickly lay down in it, and it rippled over my skin, and the bubbles came up to my neck, and I wanted to stay there forever under the blanket of bubbles, and I closed my eyes. I felt so terrible. I was so tired. I slid down lower in the hot water, and the water gurgled around my ears and I couldn't hear anything anymore, just the gurgling of the water, and I couldn't think anymore, and I didn't want to think anymore. I just wanted to lie there in the warm water, where it smelled nice and I didn't have to see anything or hear anything. How wonderful . . .

When I opened my eyes again, Laura was sitting on the edge of the bathtub. "Hello," she said. "Come out now, or you'll drown!" Her voice sounded kind, not at all mad at me. She picked me up and wrapped me in a big white towel as if I were a baby and carried me into the other room and laid me on the mattress. The room was different somehow, it smelled different, so fresh. The window was open and it was sort of dark because the curtains were closed even though it was still daytime. I felt so tired. My eyes kept on shutting. But I didn't feel sick anymore— well, only a little bit. Laura sat down next to me, picked up a book, put on her glasses, and said, "I'll read to you, would you like that?" I nodded and thought, What stupid glasses, you can't see her eyes through them at all. Then I must have fallen asleep.

## Chapter 3

When I woke up, at first I had no idea where I was. The room was pitch dark. But then it all came back, being sick and the hot bath, and I realized I'd probably slept through the whole afternoon, and now it was too late and I'd have to go back to the Home. Sunday was over. Laura was going to be fed up with me after the way I'd acted today. . . . I'd made a mess of everything, and just when Laura was being so nice and had come and sat down with me, I'd fallen asleep! How stupid can you get! Laura wouldn't want to have me anymore, that was for sure. *I* wouldn't want me either!

If I'd had a choice, I would rather not even have gotten out of bed, but of course I had to, I had to go back. So I got up and carefully opened the door and looked out, and there was Laura, sitting at the kitchen table, smoking and pounding away on the typewriter. She was working. You shouldn't bother people when they're working, but I had to. I would have knocked on the door first because that would be polite, but it's impossible to knock on a door that's already open, so I just said, "I have to go." Laura looked up right away, but she had a very absent-minded look in her eyes, so I figured that I had disturbed her. Now she wouldn't just be mad about the carpet and the messed-up rug, and because I'd been so stupid all day, but also because she had to take me back and couldn't go on doing her work. "Okay, then, get dressed," she said, and even her voice sounded absentminded.

I went to the bathroom, now that I knew where it was, and I saw Andrea's blouse, *Andrea's blouse,* the one that I had got sick all over, floating around in the bathtub. Now I wouldn't be able to smuggle it back. One more problem on top of everything else!

I put on my sweater and my jeans and my shoes and my coat, and then Miss Fielder, I mean Laura, called, "Are you ready? I'll get a taxi!"

A taxi! I'd never been in a taxi before, except once when I had to be rushed to the dentist because I had such an excruciating toothache, yet I couldn't really enjoy the ride. I couldn't enjoy it today, either. I knew we were going in a taxi so that Laura could get rid of me quickly and go back and do some more work. She probably couldn't even afford a taxi. Taxis are expensive; I knew that much. It was obvious that she was poor, because she had to work on Sundays and didn't have any real furniture or a car or even a husband, just a boyfriend.

"Are you ready? The taxi's here!" Laura called, and I sighed and came out of the bathroom and there was Laura, dressed and ready to go, and we got into the taxi. She didn't say anything, and I didn't say anything, even though I would have liked to have asked if she was fed up with me, or if I could come again the next Sunday because I'd like to very much and I was sorry about today, but I couldn't manage to get the words out. And Laura looked as if she'd rather not talk. She had a look that said, "I'm somewhere far away," almost as if she were asleep. She certainly didn't pay any attention to me. I must have been such a disappointment to her.

When we got to the Home, I got out of the taxi. Laura didn't. She stayed in it and waved and called, "Bye-bye, Jenny. See you soon!" Then the taxi drove off.

I stood there in front of the Home and looked

after the taxi, but it had already disappeared around the corner. "See you soon." What was that supposed to mean? Did she mean next Sunday, or what?

"Bye, see you next Sunday!" was not what she'd said. She'd just said, "See you soon." That sounded like "See you around." I went inside. The other children weren't all back yet, just that stupid Donny, but he was always there, and Andrea, she was back already too. The moment she saw me, she rushed up to me. Uh-oh, I thought, here it goes about the blouse, she's sure to have noticed the blouse is missing, and now it's floating around in Laura's bathtub. And who knows when I'll be able to get it back.

I had to think quickly. I could always say I didn't know anything about her blouse, and that she should be more careful about her things, or I could say I'd seen Donny take it or . . . but I didn't have a chance to think any further because Andrea already started shouting. "Come on! Tell me! How was it? Did she have a giraffe skin?"

Giraffe skin! If only she knew! I didn't say anything. I pushed past Andrea and shot up the stairs to our room and slammed the door. I wanted to be alone; I didn't want to tell her anything. The Sunday had been a disaster, but there was no need for anyone else to know, and especially not Andrea.

I should have known that Andrea would never give up. She chased me, and I managed to get the door closed before she was in the room too, demanding, "Come on! Tell me! Quickly, or else . . ."

I knew all about that "or else." If I didn't say anything, she'd really torture me, not literally, but with words, and that's even worse.

So I opened the door and said quickly, "Oh, it was fine," and "She had a polar bearskin, so there!" The part about the polar bear wasn't a lie because the shaggy white carpet really did look a little like a polar bearskin.

Andrea stared, and I quickly pushed past her and ran out to the bathroom. At least I'd be alone in there. Or so I thought, because Andrea ran after me again! I quickly locked the door, but Andrea stood outside, pounding on it.

"Dummy!" she screeched. "You've got to tell me! Does she have red hair?"

"No!" I yelled back. "Go away! She's got silver hair!"

"Liar!" shouted Andrea, rattling the door. "If you don't tell me the truth, Jenny, I'll break the door down!" She actually did start kicking the door, and it began to shudder. Andrea always gets so violent. If she went on doing it, Sister Linda would come along and be angry. I'd have to think of something, anything, just so that Andrea would have something else to think about and I would be left in peace. Suddenly I remembered that she loved reading, really loved it, was crazy about it, in fact, and that she could never get her hands on enough books . . . and Laura had told me she had written a book for children. If I told Andrea that, she'd shut up, at least for a while, and she'd leave me alone. I could even promise to bring her back a copy of Laura's book. Even though I would probably never see Laura again, there was no need to tell Andrea that, at least not today. So I called through the door, "I'll tell you something special, but you have to stop kicking the door. Promise?"

There was silence for a moment from the other side of the door, then Andrea said, "Okay, I promise."

I unlocked the door and came out. If Andrea promised, then it was all right. She could be annoying, but she never broke her promises.

"Well," I said, "if you really want to know, my Sunday Mommy writes books." "Books" was an exaggeration, but it sounded better, and Andrea couldn't disprove it.

Anyway, it worked. Andrea just stood there, open-mouthed and amazed. "Is that true, you little liar?" she asked distrustfully.

"Honest!" I said, and held up my palm. Andrea believed me then. "I'll bring you one sometime." That worked even better.

Andrea wilted. "Will you?" she asked, and I nodded. "So your Sunday Mommy is an author!" she said in an awed tone. "Some people have all the luck!"

I almost laughed. Laura, an author! She certainly wasn't that. I knew that authors were special people, and Laura wasn't special, she was just ordinary, but very nice. And I'd probably never see her again, and it was all my own fault. I wasn't going to tell Andrea that, oh, no! I'd only tell Cuddly-Bunny. I wanted to have him right then and there, to hold him tight and tell him all about it, because he'd understand. Instead the bell rang for supper. I wasn't hungry, but at least at supper I wouldn't have to talk. Andrea went in with me, and when we got to the dining hall, she whispered, "You won't forget about the book, will you?"

I nodded and thought, I won't forget, but I don't really know how I'm going to get it, either! But at least she left me alone; she now respected me because she really believed my Sunday Mommy was an author.

During supper everyone talked on and on about their great Sundays—delicious meals and what they'd seen and how they'd played. I could have told them about my day too. Today I had been out with my Sunday Foster Parent. But what a day it had been, much different from everyone else's. I decided not to say anything. I gave my cheese sandwich and my pudding to Donny. He'll eat up anything. Then finally supper was over and we were allowed to go back to our rooms. That's what I wanted to do, as quickly as I could, but suddenly there was Sister Linda next to me, saying, "You've got a phone call, Jenny." A phone call? That had never happened before. Who on earth would call me up? Sister Linda probably didn't mean it, she'd probably made a mistake, but she gave me a gentle push and said, "Hurry up, answer it!" so I went to the telephone in the hall and picked up the receiver and listened. There was no one there.

"Go on, say hello," prompted Sister Linda, and when I didn't say anything, she took the receiver from me and said, "Hello, Miss Fielder, here's Jenny."

And she handed the receiver back to me. Miss Fielder! Laura! My heart began to beat faster. I thought I was going to be sick again. What did Laura want? Probably she'd already talked to Sister Linda and complained because I'd been so bad today, and now she was going to tell me she didn't want to take me out again. Maybe she'd be mad, and I didn't know what I was going to say. I just stood there with the receiver in my hand, and I could hear someone saying, "Hello, hello," on the other end, and Sister Linda whispered, "Go on, for goodness sake, say something."

So I said, "Hello." And then Miss Fielder, I mean Laura, started talking, and her voice sounded strange, but very nice. She wasn't mad at me, not even a little.

"Hello, Jenny," she said. "I wanted to know how you were after our first Sunday." Our first Sunday, she said! And then she went on about "being patient with each other" and "getting to know one another" and "it won't take long," and she didn't say anything about the spot on the carpet. I was so happy . . . I nodded yes to everything and it didn't occur to me that she couldn't see that on the other end of the phone. How stupid I was! Then she said something really fantastic, she said, "I'm looking forward to next Sunday very much. Good-bye, you Sunday's Child!" And then there was a click. She'd put the phone down. And I just stood there with the receiver in my hand and had a really strange feeling in my stomach. I didn't feel sick anymore, just the opposite. She said she was looking forward to next Sunday! Very much! She wasn't mad at me after all, and she wanted to have me again! And she called me up especially to tell me so. The other kids never got phone calls—but I had gotten one! On the very first Sunday! How about that! I hung up the receiver carefully and went upstairs, and halfway up the stairs I remembered she'd called me Sunday's Child. I stopped. Sunday's Child! I'd been one all my life, but now I was one twice over! Because Laura would take me out each Sunday. I gave a little hop and then ran up the stairs, three at a time. I'm really good at that.

Andrea was already in our room, sitting on her bed, dangling her legs, and she asked reproachfully, "Where have you been all this time?"

And I answered as casually as I could, "If you must know, I've been on the phone with my Sunday Mommy." And then I went right to the bathroom and brushed my teeth. I didn't wash up—after all, I'd already had a bath once today—and I came back to our room and got into bed. Andrea wanted to talk, but I didn't. She kept asking things, but I shut my eyes tight, as if I were already asleep. I even started to snore, and then Andrea shut up.

But I cuddled up to Cuddly-Bunny and whispered everything into his worn-out ears. Very softly, so Andrea wouldn't hear, I told him I really didn't mind that Laura was poor and didn't have a fireplace or a car, or that she didn't look like a real mommy. She couldn't help that, she was very nice and wanted to keep me. That was the main thing. And then I made a deal with Cuddly-Bunny: The next Sunday I would be very friendly so that Laura would enjoy having me. And I bit Cuddly-Bunny's ear gently three times. That meant it was a promise. Then Cuddly-Bunny and me both fell asleep. Andrea stirred above me in her sleep. Once again, she'd refused to switch beds with me. I didn't need the top bunk anymore. I had Laura, my Sunday Mommy, and she had me!

Chapter **4**

The next day, Monday, there was a big commotion. It began the moment I woke up. Andrea was flying through our room, tearing open the closet, and pawing through our shelves, both hers and mine, muttering angrily. . . . Suddenly I realized she was looking for her blouse. I didn't say anything and just pretended I was still asleep. But I could see that Andrea kept looking at me in an accusing way. Then she even crawled under my bed so that I had to get up. I couldn't stay in bed all day anyway, I had to go to school.

So I pretended I had just woken up, and immediately Andrea ran over to me, grabbed me by my pajama top, and said ominously, "Come on, Jenny. Where is my blouse? Give it back right now!"

She couldn't possibly have known that I had borrowed it from her, so I said, "Let go of me, I haven't got it!"

"You have!" shouted Andrea, and grabbed me tighter. "I'll tell Sister Frances." What a creep! I quickly slipped my arm out of my pajama sleeve and left Andrea standing there with my pajama top in her hand without me inside it. She looked so funny I laughed, and that made her even madder. She threw the pajama top on the floor and hissed, "You thief, you give me back my blouse this minute, or I'll—" And then the bell rang for breakfast, and I hadn't even washed up!

I rushed to the bathroom with Andrea behind me, and she grabbed my toothbrush out of my hand and started to beat me on the head with it. So I picked up my washcloth—it was nice and wet—and threw it in her face. Andrea took a step backward, slipped, and sat down. It must have been really painful because she began to cry. Andrea's so sensitive.

I would have explained to her about the blouse by then, but she wouldn't let me get a word in. She had lost her temper and started to hit me, and I didn't like that.

Since she was sitting on the floor crying, I decided

to hit her just once on the head. Then she screamed even louder and bit me on the leg, really hard. You could still see her teeth marks three days later— well, two days, anyway. I was shocked and let out a piercing yell, and suddenly Sister Linda was in the bathroom, and she yelled, "That's enough, you two, stop it at once!" She grabbed both of us, and Andrea sobbed loudly and I cried, though without any tears, and rubbed my leg. Sister Linda told Andrea to go to breakfast and sent me to our room to get dressed. "I don't want to hear another word!" she said. So once more there was no chance to explain. At breakfast Andrea kept glaring at me furiously. I just stirred my oatmeal fixedly and stuck my nose deep into my mug of cocoa. She should have stopped crying about her stupid blouse.

After breakfast Andrea was the first to leave, and she ran off to our room. I followed along slowly because I had to get my school bag. I took as long as I could, because I didn't really want to meet Andrea again. But I did meet her—she nearly knocked me over. "I've looked everywhere!" she shouted. "Everywhere! The blouse isn't in our room!" And she looked at me closely and said, "Honest, cross your heart and hope to die, do you have my blouse?" I shook my head, I really *didn't* have it, but I couldn't cross my heart.

But Andrea didn't notice that, she just ran off, saying, "Then that stupid Donny must have it. Just wait till I get him!" Well, I knew, of course, that he didn't have it. Now she'd give him a hard time and she still wouldn't find the blouse. She might pinch him and pull his hair, and there'd be nothing he could do about it . . . but then I thought, He'll survive. He's so stupid, anyway.

But I didn't feel too happy about the whole thing, and I promised myself that next Sunday I would make sure I brought the blouse back and I'd smuggle it into our room. And I'd give Donny a present or something. Then again, maybe I wouldn't. Maybe I'd just play with him a little; that would be cheaper.

I took my school things and quickly slipped out of the room. In the hall I stopped and listened to see whether I could hear Donny crying because Andrea had caught up with him, but I didn't hear anything, so I quickly went to school.

That afternoon when I came home, there was still more trouble. Andrea had told on me. She had told Sister Frances that she was suspicious of me, and I had to go to Sister Frances's room and explain even the reason why the blouse was now floating around in Laura's bathtub. Sister Frances was very mad and said I was a deceitful little girl and she wouldn't stand for it, and that poor Donny had had to suffer because of my lies, and so on.

I was pretty ashamed, but also pretty annoyed. I hadn't stolen the blouse; I had just borrowed it. I couldn't help it if Andrea was the kind of person who didn't lend things. And I didn't see why they made me tell them about throwing up, since that had nothing to do with it.

But I didn't say anything like that, I just told them I was going to bring the blouse back. Then Sister Frances said the most terrible thing of all. She said she would have to consider whether, under the circumstances, she could let me go out with Miss Fielder again. She didn't say under which circumstances exactly. I stood there speechless, just looking at my feet.

So that was that. Now she wouldn't let me go out with Laura ever again. Just when I had begun to look forward to it. I thought that was really mean. There was a tight knot of anger in my stomach.

Sister Frances sent me out and I left, slamming the door behind me. So she called me back in and I had to go out again, this time shutting the door quietly. I was supposed to apologize to Andrea and to Donny too. But that I refused to do. Never! It was all Andrea's fault, anyway, and I'd never say I was sorry to Donny. He was much too stupid.

What I really wanted to do was smash something or kick in Sister Frances's door! But I didn't have the nerve.

I ran back to our room and threw myself on my bed, even though it was only noon, and I held Cuddly-Bunny tight and was so mad, I couldn't even talk to him. They were all mean and unfair! All of them except Laura. And now I'd never be allowed to visit her again. Out of pure anger I bit Cuddly-Bunny's ear hard. He couldn't help it, but the others could! All of them! I wouldn't stay here any longer! I'd get out. I'd just run away to Laura. I'd take Cuddly-Bunny, put on my coat because it was cold, and run away right after lunch. First I'd go on the subway, then I'd go down the long gray street, then around the corner, and I'd be there. I'd ring the bell, and she'd open the door and she'd be really pleased. I would tell her everything because it wasn't my fault. If she wasn't there, I'd just sit down on the steps and wait, and she'd come sometime. When she saw me sitting there, she'd open her arms, and I'd jump up and put my arms around her neck and . . . But I'd need a token to get on the subway, and I didn't have any allowance to buy one.

Andrea always had money, I don't know how she managed it. She was sure to have some allowance left. But how could I ask her if she'd lend me money? She never, never would. And especially not now!

The best thing to do would be just to call Laura up. She'd come and get me. Now, this minute. Then I realized I didn't know her phone number. Sister Frances would know it, but she wouldn't tell me, that was for sure. And the phone book was in her room, so I couldn't just waltz in and look it up. She was bound to catch me, she always caught me, I knew that much. She'd also catch me if I tried to run away, and she'd forbid me to go, and she'd make me stay in the Home every Sunday forever and ever.

So then I began to cry. I couldn't help it. The tears just came. It didn't help even when I pressed Cuddly-Bunny into my eyes. The tears kept falling and ran all over his checked trousers. Suddenly I felt something next to me, something scratching under my quilt, near my ear. I held Cuddly-Bunny closer and slid deep down under the quilt. There was someone there, and I didn't want there to be anyone there. But the scratching went on, and a hand was pushed under the quilt and it found my head and it scratched. "Go away," I said under the quilt, but the hand didn't hear, it just kept on scratching. It wasn't Andrea. She didn't scratch, she pinched.

I pushed the quilt to one side and saw it was Donny standing by my bed with his hand in my hair. That stupid Donny! What did he want? "Beat it!" I hissed. And my voice sounded muffled. Probably because I'd been crying.

But Donny didn't beat it, he looked at me with his wide-open eyes and drooled a bit, and the saliva ran down his chin, and he began to stroke my cheeks where the tears had run. "Cwying," he said and shook his head. He fumbled in his pockets and pulled out some hard candy and offered it to me. It was very sticky, with pieces of fluff stuck to it, and he expected me to take it! Before I could shake my head, he had stuffed it into my mouth and grinned delightedly, and then he lifted up my quilt and slipped in next to me and began to pat my cheeks again. What a strange kid! He'd never done that before. He shouldn't be doing it now, either!

But somehow I couldn't make myself push him out of bed. I was so weak—inside, I mean. Donny snuggled up close to me, he was warm and much smaller than me, and he was stroking me, and the stroking felt very nice . . . and the candy was nice too. I moved over a little, so that Donny had more room, but he moved over too and somehow kicked my ankle with his dirty shoes, and he laughed and didn't even drool. His face was close to mine. He had opened his eyes wide and they were very blue, just like the sky in summer. I'd never seen Donny's eyes so close up. On his nose there were three freckles, exactly three. I'd never seen those before either. I gulped. Donny had just crawled into my bed and now he was making me feel better. Even though he was usually so stupid, he wasn't being stupid now at all. Suddenly I thought I should apologize to him because I'd gotten him in trouble with Andrea about the blouse. Right now, when no one else could hear, I would just say that I was sorry.

I took a deep breath and said softly, "I'm sorry." Donny didn't answer, he had closed his eyes and snuggled up close and now he was stroking my face. "Hey, you," I said and tickled him under his chin, "I'm sorry."

Just then the door burst open and Andrea ran in and stopped in front of my bed, squealed, "Aha!" and tore the quilt off us with excitement, hooting,

"A pair of lovebirds, a pair of lovebirds, ha, ha, ha, ha!"

Stupid jerk! She had no idea, she just didn't have a clue. Lovebirds! What a stupid thing to say! Donny had wanted to comfort me. There was no need for her to act like that. Suddenly I wanted to get away. I wanted to get out.

I pushed Donny away and jumped up, and Andrea stood there in front of me, hooting and giggling, so I punched her in the stomach really hard. I didn't care. I just wanted to get out, and Andrea should have let me go. So I punched her again. Andrea's eyes almost popped out. She gasped for air and grabbed her stomach where I'd punched her. Then she fell to the floor, writhed around, and let out the most terrible screams. I stood where I was, shocked. I couldn't really have punched her that hard, could I? Andrea didn't stop screaming or writhing, she acted as if I'd killed her. But if you can writhe and scream, then you can't be killed, can you!

Then Donny began to cry too, and it was all my fault.

Suddenly Sister Frances stood in the doorway and she rushed into the room, grabbed Andrea, pulled her to her feet, and asked, "Where does it hurt?"

Andrea pointed to her stomach, and Sister Frances felt it and massaged it. She didn't look at me, only at Donny, who was howling, and Andrea, who was sobbing. At last Andrea stopped crying. She pointed at me and tried to say something, but she never managed to because Sister Frances said something instead: "Come with me, all three of you!" She took Donny by the hand and went out. Andrea and I followed after her. You don't argue with Sister Frances.

We had just reached Sister Frances's room when Andrea started talking again, saying that I had punched her to the floor, and . . . and . . .

"I don't want to hear another word!" Sister Frances said. "I've had enough for today." She took a long hard look at the three of us. And then she shook her head. "Children, children, why do you have to fight, why can't you manage just one day without fighting?"

Donny began to cry again, and Andrea started too and pointed at me. "It's all Jenny's fault!" I just stood there and wished I had run away.

"Quiet!" said Sister Frances. "I've seen enough tears for today. If you keep this up, you'll put the rain out of work." She pointed to the window. It

wasn't just raining, it was pouring cats and dogs. If
I was going to run away now, I'd need an umbrella,
and I didn't have one. Darn!

Sister Frances had noticed something. Could she
read my mind? All she said was, "Now, let's just sit
down for a while and we'll all have some cocoa."
She looked at me closely while she said it, got four
cups and a box of cookies, poured hot milk and
cocoa into a pitcher, and set it all on the table. Donny
and Andrea had stopped bawling. They were
amazed. No one had ever heard of having cocoa with
Sister Frances. Donny reached for his cup right away
and reached into the box of cookies and stuffed his
mouth full. Andrea sniffled for a while, then she
helped herself too. Meanwhile, I sat at the table
and just couldn't figure out what it all meant. I was
certain that I was going to be punished, but when
and what punishment?

Sister Frances said nothing about it, she just said
to me, "You like cocoa, don't you?" and I thought
she was winking at me while she said it. But I must
have imagined it. Then she put Donny on her lap,
poured cocoa, and asked us if we would like to play
a game. We all stared at each other. . . . Andrea could
almost look at me normally again. Play a game? Of
course we'd like to play a game. But with Sister

Frances? She usually never played with us, only at Christmastime or when someone had a birthday.

"Well?" asked Sister Frances, rocking Donny backward and forward on her lap. Donny was grinning happily, his mouth stuffed full.

"Let's play War!" cried Andrea, and I nodded. She jumped up and said, "I'll get the cards, I'll go!" and rushed out of the room. Andrea is always so violent.

So then we sat around the table and played. Donny won a lot because Sister Frances was helping him, so that didn't really count, but Donny is still so little, you have to help him. He was always so happy when he managed to say "war."

Andrea had a very red face from bending low over the table so she could say "war" as fast as possible. I tried hard too, but somehow I wasn't as quick as usual that day. I think I know why. Maybe I really wanted Andrea to win because if I let her win, it was a little like apologizing.

Andrea didn't realize this, of course, she looked scornfully at me and said, "Jeepers, you're slow today!" But Sister Frances realized what was going on, I think. She watched me thoughtfully as I kept losing and didn't get mad.

When the fourth game was over, Sister Frances

put her hand on my shoulder and said, "As a matter of fact, I've given next Sunday some thought, you know." I did know and my heart began to beat faster. "I think," said Sister Frances, and her hand stayed on my shoulder, "I think we'll give it another try, Jenny."

I knew what she meant. I would be allowed out again with Laura! Sister Frances wasn't angry with me anymore, and I wasn't going to be punished! "Off you go, my dears," she said, pushing Donny gently from her lap, then she picked up the cards and took us to the door of her room. "I can't while away the whole afternoon with you all!" And then she laughed, put a finger to her lips, and whispered, "Not a word about this, do you hear? Or else I'll have to spend every afternoon from now on playing with naughty children!"

We laughed too, a little bit. It actually wasn't such a bad idea. From now on, Sister Frances would sit in her room and instead of always cleaning up after us and scolding us, she'd play War and lose all the time. . . . I'd lost too on purpose, but in return I was again friends with Andrea. I might even become friends with Donny now. All that cuddling earlier today had really surprised me and made me feel better, so I decided I'd play with him once in a while, if I had time. And I would be allowed to go to Laura's again next Sunday. A promise is a promise.

I decided I would be really good for the whole rest of the week. Right up until Sunday, so that Sister Frances wouldn't change her mind.

Chapter **5**

Well, Sister Frances didn't change her mind. I watched her carefully the whole week, and she never mentioned it. But I was very well behaved just in case. I had even apologized to Andrea. She hadn't let me forget it, of course; she insisted I apologize, so I did. It was actually very simple.

I hardly saw Donny during the week. I didn't really want to see him. I felt very strange about him. All the time I pretended that I had a lot of homework to do and didn't have time to play with him. I felt a little sorry for him because at every meal he would slide up close to me and stare at me with his big blue eyes, and I knew that he wanted something. But at least I always gave him half of my bread, and some of my cereal at breakfast. So he was happy about that; Donny's such a pig.

And then it was Sunday, and there I was, sitting in the hall, waiting for Laura. The moment I got up, Andrea told me not to forget the blouse or the book I had promised her. She'd said the same thing every morning that week, so I knew it by heart. I certainly wouldn't forget. There was no reason for her to go on and on.

She'd already left. Her Sunday Parents had picked her up earlier. She told me she was going on a special trip today, and now she was gone. Maybe my Sunday Mommy would take me on a special trip today too. That would be fantastic, but anything would be fine with me. Today I was going to be very polite and good.

It was already five after nine. Laura still wasn't here. Where could she be? She had been late last Sunday too, maybe she would always come late. It didn't matter, I'd just wait for her. She'd be sure to pick me up. After all, she had said on the telephone that she was looking forward to next Sunday. Next Sunday was today, and so she would come and pick me up. I just knew it. There was no doubt about it, but just in case I clenched my thumb into my fist. That would bring me luck. Now nothing could go wrong.

Anyway, if Laura didn't come and pick me up

today, she'd really be missing something because I'd made up my mind to be so polite and good. Neither Laura's smoking nor that funny apartment would bother me a bit. And if she had to work at her table in the workshop-kitchen, looking absentminded, I would be quiet as a mouse and make her a cup of coffee. I'm good at that. And then I'd clean up for her. Everything was so messy, she probably just didn't have any time to clean up. She'd be very pleased and would think I was wonderful. Now if only she would come so that I could start helping her.

And suddenly there she was in front of me in her windbreaker and boy's rubber hat. I hadn't seen her come in. I slid off my seat, and she held out her hand and took mine and said, "Well, Sunday's Child? Shall we go?" and she led me to the door.

There she was at last! I had made up my mind to be really polite and to say, "Good morning, Laura, it's nice to see you!" But once again I couldn't get the words out. How stupid can you be?

Out on the street, Laura put an arm easily around my shoulders and gave me a squeeze, just once quickly. That felt nice. And she ruffled my hair. I don't really like people ruffling my hair, but I let Laura do it. While she did, she looked at me with her great big Cuddly-Bunny eyes, Cuddly-Bunny eyes that today weren't spoiled by those stupid glasses, and she smiled and said, "Well, old thing? It's good to see you too." But again I said nothing. I just had a nice warm feeling in my stomach, as if I had said it.

Laura put her arm around my shoulders again and we walked off side by side. That didn't work too well because Laura took such big steps and I had to take two little ones to keep up. It was like a walking race. Laura noticed and took her arm away and took my hand and held it high and asked, "Are you too big to hold hands?" And she held both our hands high. I shook my head quickly. It was nice holding hands, even if I was much too big for it.

"Okay, then," said Laura, keeping my hand in her hand, and off we went. Now our steps matched perfectly. And so we walked down the street hand in hand toward the subway station. I could have walked like that forever.

"I thought we'd go on a trip today. Would you like that, Jenny?" asked Laura, and she squeezed my hand, and I squeezed back. Not hard, just so that she'd notice. A trip. Great!

But suddenly I realized that she didn't have a car, so how was she going to take me on an outing?

All the other children went on outings by car. So I said, "Without a car?"

Right away I was mad at myself. I knew that she couldn't afford a car. Cars are expensive. How stupid of me.

But Laura wasn't at all angry. "We don't need one," she said, pulling me along. "We can go on a trip without a car, don't you think?" I nodded, relieved. "We'll go by subway. To a lake," she said. "I thought we could have a picnic, or is it too cold for you?"

I shook my head hard even though it was pretty cold. The only time I'd gone on a picnic was once with the other kids and Sister Linda. And that was in the park, not by a lake. Was there really a lake in the city? It didn't matter. I think even if Laura had suggested that we sit down at the subway stop and eat bread and honey, I would have enjoyed it, just because she was there.

We got to the station platform and Laura let go of my hand. Too bad, I thought, it was nice holding hands. But once we were in the train she sat down next to me and took my hand again, and she held it for the entire trip. She looked sideways at me from time to time. I didn't look at her and I didn't say anything, either. She must have thought I was stupid or something, but I didn't know what to say. It was as if my mouth was nailed shut, but it was better not to say anything than to say something silly.

A fat lady sat down opposite us. She had a bulging shopping bag between her legs and she was staring down at it. I thought, What bad luck it would have been if she were my Sunday Mommy. She wouldn't have held my hand on her lap, she would have been busy guarding her shopping bag. I liked Laura much better, I knew that much. If only she'd let her hair grow. That wouldn't hurt her, and she wouldn't look so much like a boy. Maybe I'd tell her, someday. . . .

We traveled for a long time, and when we got out, we weren't in the city anymore. There were just meadows and bushes and trees here and there, and the lake. It wasn't a particularly big lake, you could easily see the other side, but even so it was a lake. There were even ducks swimming on it. "Here we are!" said Laura. She pulled the rubber hat off her head, stuffed it in her windbreaker pocket, shook her stubbly head, and raced off. "Beat you to the water!" I took my hat off too, put it in my coat pocket, and raced after her. Laura was already quite a way ahead; she ran very fast for a grown-up. Her windbreaker billowed in the wind and her rubber hat fell out of her pocket, but she didn't notice. She ran on and reached the shore and crowed, "I won!"

What a silly person she was! I picked up her hat and ran over and said, "Hey, that doesn't count. You didn't say 'on your mark, get set, go.' You always have to say that if you're going to race, otherwise it's not fair." Suddenly I realized I had spoken to her like a friend—it was so natural.

Laura didn't seem to have noticed anything, she just sat in the wet grass, grinning at me. "You're absolutely right. But I wanted to win!"

She pulled me down beside her on the wet ground. Then she took the rubber hat from me and crammed it down over my nose so I couldn't see anything. "I won, go on, admit it!" she said and gave me a shove so hard, I nearly fell over.

"But . . ." I said, and then I had to laugh. I pulled the hat off so I could see again and put it on Laura's head. There! Now she couldn't see anything, either. I wanted to give her a shove too, to make her fall over, but I didn't have the nerve.

Laura sat very still with the hat pulled down over her nose. For a minute I thought she was angry. It wasn't right to act like that with grown-ups. Who knows what would have happened if I'd ever pulled a hat down over Sister Frances's nose! What a thought!

Laura wasn't angry, though. She kept the hat on her head and looked like a bank robber on TV, and she shook her head this way and that and mumbled something that sounded muffled, something that sounded like "Shit!"

Had she really said "shit"? I would never say that, not out loud at least. If Sister Frances ever heard me say such a thing, she'd never let me go with Laura again. But I really did have a Sunday Mommy who said "shit"!

Laura pulled the hat off her head with a jerk and said, "Shit—I left the picnic at home!"

I had to giggle, because she looked so furious about it. Furious at herself, not at me. I couldn't do anything about it. It didn't matter anyway, and it could have happened to anyone. I hardly ever forget anything, but other people do. Laura was a scatterbrain. I wanted to reassure her, but I just said, "I'm not hungry, anyway."

"Well, I am!" shouted Laura, and jumped up. I thought it was really kind that she had a picnic so early this morning. A picnic for me! Even though it was still sitting in the kitchen and here we were at the lake.

"Race you to the hot dog man!" cried Laura. "On your mark, get set, go!" The hot dog man was right over on the other side, so you almost had to go around the whole lake.

She ran off and once again dropped her rubber hat on the ground. I picked it up and ran after her. She really was forgetful. She needed to be taken care of. But first of all I'd have to catch up to her. She could run fast, but I could run faster. I was good at running, and I wanted to show her. The meadow was wet and squishy, the lake was big . . . and Laura had a good head start. But I'd catch up to her. I ran and began to feel hot; I ran faster and got a pain in my side, but that didn't matter. I wanted to run as fast as I could so Laura would see how fast I could run. I passed her, and I could see she was already panting. I raced on, and the meadow seemed to skim past under my feet. I felt as if I only had to take a big jump and I'd be flying. I'd fly straight to the hot dog man, grab some hot dogs in midair, double back to Laura, and call, "Hey! Catch these!" and I'd drop the hot dogs on top of her and then I'd land next to her and she'd be absolutely amazed! A girl who could fly and hot dogs from heaven!

Was it really impossible to fly? I hopped a little hop as I ran, but my legs came right back to earth and I kept running. I guess I could only fly in my imagination. Too bad. And then there I was at the hot dog man. Laura was miles behind me, well, yards, anyway. She held her sides and called over to me, "Hungry!" And she gasped for air. I grinned secretly. Grown-ups aren't supposed to run like that, they just can't do it. Poor Laura. "Hot dogs!" she said to the hot dog man, still wheezing. "With lots of mustard!"

We sat on a bench in front of the hot dog man and ate two hot dogs each. I was hungry after all. When we had finished, Laura bought some more hot dogs, and mustard got smeared on our chins, and I secretly wiped my greasy fingers on my jacket. Then we were full, sitting next to each other on the bench, saying nothing, just looking at the lake.

The ducks were swimming around, quacking. There weren't any ducklings. I guessed they hadn't hatched yet. There were just Mommy-ducks and Daddy-ducks. Two of them were swimming very close together. Maybe they'd soon have babies, I thought. They looked as if they'd like some. They were very sweet to each other. If they did have babies, they'd keep them with them forever. They wouldn't give them away to an orphanage for ducklings, because there wasn't such a thing for ducks. Only humans needed things like that. Why? Ducks managed much better. . . . If we had bread with us,

I would have liked to have fed the ducks. But we didn't have any bread, just greasy fingers.

"A penny for your thoughts!" said Laura suddenly and leaned forward. "What are you thinking about?" And she said it as if she really was interested in knowing. Should I tell her about the ducks? I wondered. I didn't know how to. Better not. I could always tell her later.

At that moment fat gray rain clouds began to loom up in the sky. "I was thinking," I said quickly, pointing at the sky, "that I was sitting up there on that cloud." She'd probably think I was crazy, but I didn't know what else to say.

Laura looked up at the clouds. "And I'm thinking," she said, "that I'm sitting up on that other cloud, waving at you. Can you see me?"

Of course I couldn't, I'd just said that about the cloud off the top of my head. Laura had taken me seriously. She was like that. So I said, "Of course I can. I can see you. I'm going to give my cloud a little push with my feet. So that it comes over to yours."

That wasn't bad, and Laura immediately picked up the thread. "And I'm trying to stand up on my cloud so I can see better," she said. "But it's tricky. Do you see how the cloud's wobbling under my feet? I'm going to lose my balance. Whoops! I'm going down onto the cloud again! I know what I'll do. I'll pull out my cloud until it's all long and thin like a rope, and I'll throw it over to your side. And the rope will tie itself to your cloud, and I'll scamper across like a monkey and call, 'Wait, here I come!' And I'll sit down next to you."

"Just like we are here," I said and looked at Laura.

And Laura looked at me. "I'll let the rope, the cloud rope, fall—it's falling into the middle of the lake, can you see it?" She pointed to the lake.

I could see it. I honestly could. The lake had ripples as if something really had fallen in. "And I'll jump down from my cloud," I said, "and dive into the lake to get your rope. How about that?"

Laura laughed and gave me a squeeze. "Oh, leave the rope. We'll come swimming here in the summer, I promise. I'd rather you stayed here with me. Up on the cloud!" And suddenly her voice was different. She wasn't laughing anymore. She said seriously, "Would you like that?"

Of course I would. What a question! And I'd like to come swimming too in the summer. It was a long time till summer. There were a whole bunch of Sundays to go when we would do things together, go on trips and things. Laura wanted to, I knew that now, and I wanted to. My stomach started to tingle. When summer was over, we'd still keep on doing things. For years and years . . . My stomach got even more tingly, and the tingles went up to my throat. But it wasn't like the time that the sugary tea wanted to come up. This was like happiness that wanted to bubble out. My Laura. Mine. From now on, every Sunday forever.

Then suddenly I began to tell her things. I was amazed at myself, but it was really pretty easy. It was as if I were telling Andrea, but a nice, friendly Andrea, not one who pinched and never stopped talking. Suddenly I couldn't understand why I hadn't told Laura anything before.

She was like me, only a little bit different. I told her everything, and she listened quietly and opened her great big Cuddly-Bunny eyes wide. I told her about him first of all, and she didn't laugh at me. She thought it was perfectly normal to have a Cuddly-Bunny. She even asked what Cuddly-Bunny looked like. Then I told her about school, and that I liked gym, but otherwise it wasn't that great. And I told her about the Home, especially about last Monday, when there had been that scene and Andrea had been so mean to me. Laura said that it had been her fault too because she should have called Sister Frances about the blouse, and then there wouldn't have been a problem. But she said that next time I really should ask Andrea if I want to borrow something of hers. That sounded like a good idea, but then Laura didn't know Andrea. So I told her about Donny, and how stupid we all thought he was, except that I didn't think he was so stupid anymore. Then Laura said it often happened like that. If you took the trouble to look at people closely, most of them weren't so stupid as you'd thought. She was right because on Monday I had looked very closely at Donny and had seen his freckles and his sky-blue eyes, and now he seemed different to me than he had before.

Then I told her that I'd cried and how I'd wanted to run away to her. Laura looked very serious and said I must never, ever do that, because running away usually didn't end well. It would make everyone worry a lot and anyway, there was no need for me to. She would pick me up every Sunday, that was all arranged and promised. If I wanted, she would swear always to come. I said she didn't need to because Sister Frances had turned out to be very understanding. She'd let me come this Sunday and had even played with us. When she heard that, Laura said, "You see!" I wanted to ask her what she meant, but then some raindrops splashed down on us. Our clouds weren't clouds for sitting on anymore, they were just ordinary rain clouds.

Laura jumped up and our conversation was over. "Hurry up," she cried. So I jumped up too and buttoned her windbreaker, one button after the other, so that she wouldn't get wet. Laura stood there and let me, she didn't pull away even though it took me a long time and we were both getting wet. She smiled all along, and her cheeks got red and she put her hands on my head for a moment—cold hands, but they made me feel warm. Then she buttoned up my coat, one button after the other. She buttoned it up wrong, the top button was left over. But that didn't matter. Then we held hands and ran off to the subway. The rain beat down on our heads because we had forgotten to put our hats on. We ran home. Not to the Home, but home to Laura's house. Sunday wasn't over. Not for ages yet. Fantastic. I didn't want this Sunday ever to end—at least not till next Sunday. And then it could start all over again.

# Chapter 6

The trip home went incredibly fast. The rain just poured down on us. It didn't bother us in the train, of course, but when we got out at Laura's street, we really got soaked. My hair hung down like wet string, and Laura's looked like wet feathers. We'd been so busy talking that we forgot to put our hats on. And I forgot to look where we were going. I meant to memorize the way, just in case. . . .

Laura's apartment stunk of smoke again. I knew it would. I didn't like this smoking business, and I'd tell her so one day. I didn't have the nerve yet. Smoking is really bad for you, it can make you sick. And I certainly didn't want Laura to get sick. She might die, and we were only just getting to know one another.

I went straight to the workshop-kitchen and

opened the window. There and in the white room too. The workshop-kitchen was a mess again. I decided I had to start cleaning it up right away. Laura was such a slob. The dishes weren't washed, ashtrays weren't emptied, paper was scattered all over the table, and right in the middle of everything stood a plastic shopping bag with our picnic in it—the one she'd forgotten.

I was just wondering where to start cleaning when Laura called from the bathroom. I had to come immediately and take a bath, she said. Otherwise we'd both catch cold because we'd gotten so wet, and if I caught cold, they'd be upset at the Home.

She was right. I didn't want to get a cold, I always look so awful with a red nose and swollen eyes. It was a cold like that that had frightened away those Sunday Parents ages ago.

I could clean up later, the mess wouldn't run away. I went into the bathroom and there stood Laura completely naked. I was really pretty shocked. I looked at her and then looked away again.

"Get undressed and get in with me," said Laura, and she wasn't at all embarrassed. She stood there without any clothes on, bending over the edge of the tub, sloshing the water around. I only hoped she'd put a lot of bubble bath in so that we wouldn't be able to see each other too well.

She did put some in, from a tube, and then she splashed it around so that it made lots of bubbles, and then she got in and said I should get in too. It looked wonderful, even though I felt a little strange. I had never taken a bath with a woman before. Only with Andrea, and even that was a long time ago.

In fact, there weren't enough bubbles, I could still see Laura in the water—her head and her neck and her breasts. She actually had breasts. I had never noticed them before because she always wore such big, baggy sweaters.

I know that all women have breasts and that one day even I will have them. Sister Frances has super-breasts—really big and unmistakable. But Laura's were smaller. I looked away again quickly and began to get undressed. Otherwise I'd just be standing in the bathroom, looking stupid.

Laura was splashing around happily in the bath, making "Ohhh!" and "Ahhh!" noises. Then she rummaged around and out of a little basket she pulled lots of bath animals and little boats. She wound them up and suddenly little animals and boats were all bobbing among the bubbles. They rattled about, knocked into one another, and over-turned. One of them was a Donald Duck. He could only swim backward. He looked so funny as he paddled backward in his sailor suit. His beak stuck out of the water and collided with Laura's breasts. Laura screeched and I had to laugh. Then I realized I had nothing on and I jumped into the bath, as quick as a flash, because I felt cold.

And then we sailed the boats and the little animals together. I let Donald Duck bump into my breasts—not that I really have any, of course.

Then Laura tickled the soles of my feet with her toes and I tickled her feet with my toes, and then our toes started to wiggle at each other and there was a mass of tickly toes. Laura got the giggles. She dabbed gently at my big toe with her big toe and said, "Hello, you! That's a toe-kiss!" I dabbed my big toe against hers and kissed back. Then we both started giggling so hard that we fell over into the water, under the bubbles.

We came up again at the same moment, spitting out water and gasping for air, and Laura climbed out of the bathtub and announced, "I'm hungry!"

Again? I thought. We'd just had all those hot dogs.

Pieces of foam hung all over her body. She looked as though she had been splotched with white, and on her head she had a blob of foam like a crown. She ran out of the bathroom, dripping wet and naked, and before I could figure out what she was doing, she came back and hopped into the bath with a plastic shopping bag on her outstretched arm. Our picnic! She plunked it down on the bathroom floor and began to unpack it. Sandwiches, apples, bananas, chocolate—she put everything out on the slippery edge of the bath. Immediately one banana slid into the water. I caught it, and Laura held out a ham sandwich for me.

I had never before eaten a ham sandwich in the bathtub. At the Home all our eating is done at the table.

It tasted good. Laura thought so too. In fact, we ate up the whole picnic. We threw the banana peels and apple cores overboard. We could clean them up later. I would do it, since Laura was sure to forget. She was lying back in the bath, munching and splashing around in the warm water, grinning at me. We shared the last piece of chocolate. Then Laura got out and grabbed the towel. I recognized it from the last Sunday. I got out too and we rubbed each other dry, till we were both red and tingly. I wasn't embarrassed anymore that we were naked. It just didn't occur to me. Laura put on a long white bathrobe, and she put a nightgown on me. It was white too, with little blue flowers. It was much too long and hung down over my feet, and it wasn't even time for bed. It was still light, but the nightgown was nice and comforting and it smelled so nice, of Laura. In the Home we all have pajamas. Nighties are much nicer. Everything at Laura's is much nicer.

She put her arm around me and we wandered into the white room. We sat on the mattress with its tasseled rug. Laura pulled the white curtains closed. "To shut out this gray old day," she said and pulled a woolly blanket over us both. Neither of us wanted to catch cold. We sat under the blanket as if it were a tent. Only our heads stuck out. I slid nearer to Laura, she put her arm around me again, and I felt her chest against my cheek. It was soft like Cuddly-Bunny's but much softer.

Laura rocked me back and forth. I think I was grinning just like Donny had on Monday on Sister Frances's lap. It was nice to be rocked. I wanted it to go on forever. *Forever.*

And suddenly, I don't know how it happened, I said to Laura's chest, because it was still pressed softly against my cheek, "Couldn't you keep me here with you?"

Laura stopped rocking me . . . and then the telephone rang. Just at that exact moment. Laura jumped, and so did I, because I was lying on her arm. She let go of me immediately, jumped up, ran out, and closed the door behind her.

And there I was, sitting alone on the mattress. It was suddenly much colder than it had been. I sighed. Always, whenever there's something important, you get disturbed. Laura hadn't answered me yet. She had to go to the telephone. I wondered who she was talking to.

I was sure she'd come back right away, sure she'd say to the person on the phone that she couldn't talk now because I was there and had just asked her something. I tried to listen, but I couldn't hear anything because the door was shut. I sighed and stood up. It was no fun sitting by myself on the mattress. It was so lonely.

I could clean up. After all, I had told myself I'd do that. But now I didn't feel like it, and anyway, in this room the mess was not so bad. It didn't matter that there were a lot of books lying around. It looked pretty. I kicked at a book with my foot. When was Laura coming back, for goodness sake?

I was bored. Maybe I would put the books together. Then it would look nicer. I began to pile them up—the big ones with the big ones, the little ones with the little ones. That made two high towers of books. They looked bright and colorful. Maybe they'd look even nicer if I arranged them by color. So I took the towers apart and sorted out the books with blue covers, and then the ones with red and the ones with green and the ones with lots of different colors. Now there were four piles, smaller ones. Maybe one tall tower of books would be nicest. I piled up the books one on top of another again and the tower tottered. Then Laura called, "Come into the kitchen and we'll play a game." Finally, she had finished her telephone call. But why did we have to play a game? I thought we were going to talk some more and cuddle. I would rather talk and cuddle.

I went into the kitchen. Laura was sitting at the table. She had pushed the papers to one side and put out a Monopoly board. She looked up at me, and right away I could see that she had that faraway look again. Would she rather be working? But then she wouldn't have set up the game. There would be no more talking and cuddling, that was for sure. Now it was time to play, but I didn't feel like it. Grownups always think that children like playing games. It isn't always true.

I sat down with her and we began. It was no fun at all. Laura just didn't play right. She made the dumbest mistakes. She moved my piece instead of hers, she shook the dice impatiently, and when I cheated, she didn't notice anything even though it was so obvious even Donny would have spotted it. She played as though her mind were on something else. Not on the game, not even on me. I could see it in her face. What was the matter? I kept on winning, but it wasn't any fun because she was playing so stupidly. So I just stopped. If she was going to be the way she was now, I didn't like it. It couldn't be that she was mad at me. I hadn't done anything bad today.

And then suddenly I realized. It wasn't me, it was the person who had called. Until then she'd been nice, and now she was strange. Stupid person to call. I got angry. I picked up the dice and threw them on the floor and threw my paper money after them. The game was stupid. The person on the telephone was stupid. Sunday was stupid now too.

Laura looked up; she had finally noticed that I was there. She looked at me with her wide-open eyes and said nothing, just bent down and picked up the paper money. She couldn't find the dice. I could see them, they had rolled under the shelf, but I didn't tell her. Let her go on looking! She was stupid too!

But then I felt sorry for her, crawling around the kitchen floor on her hands and knees, looking and not getting angry that I'd been so wild. I would have liked to apologize now, but once again I couldn't get the words out. I got up, reached under the shelf, and picked up the stupid dice and held them out to her. Laura took my hand and still said nothing, but she looked at me like she had before in the bathtub and on the mattress. Laura was Laura again.

So then I told her everything—that I didn't like her to be on the phone for so long, and that she hadn't noticed that I straightened up the books for her into a tower, and that she had played really pathetically and that, anyway, I didn't want to play, and that I had asked her a question and she hadn't answered me, and now Sunday was almost over and I'd have to go back to the Home. And I didn't want to. Not now, so soon. And anyway . . .

Laura listened to all of it. She held my hand with the dice still in it. Then she told me she was sad that the telephone had disturbed us. It had been Chris, her boyfriend. He had wanted to take her out for dinner, and she couldn't go because I was there. She was glad that I was there, but Chris didn't like it, he wanted to have her all to himself, and now she didn't know how it had gotten so complicated, or how it would all work out.

So that was it. At least I knew what was going on now. She should have told me all that right away. Laura looked all crumpled in her bathrobe. I felt sorry for her because Chris was so stupid and had gotten her upset. He shouldn't do that. He was jealous that Laura wanted to be with me. She had told him that. I thought that was really nice of her. Now I didn't mind at all that she'd said nothing about the tower of books or that she'd messed up the game. She was sad because that stupid Chris was jealous of me.

I went up close to her and told her she shouldn't worry, she had me now.

"Yes, you're right," said Laura and laughed wryly, then she was happy again all of a sudden. Laura was like that.

She put away the game, I helped her with it, and then we made ourselves some hot cocoa, with real cocoa, not the kind when you just mix chocolate into milk. We mixed real cocoa powder and sugar together, Laura poured some milk into it, and I stirred it into a brown paste. Then we poured it into a pot of hot milk and both of us stirred so it wouldn't burn on the bottom.

But it did burn because just while we were stirring, the phone rang again. I quickly grabbed Laura's bathrobe. She shouldn't go to the phone. It would probably be Chris again and she'd just get upset. "Don't answer it," I said and held on to her and forgot to stir, and Laura forgot too, and then the cocoa boiled over. It hissed and smelled, and the telephone rang and rang like crazy.

I held on to the corner of Laura's bathrobe. The cocoa was ruined, but I didn't care. The main thing was that she shouldn't go to the phone. Laura gave a deep sigh. "Another disaster!" she said. Then she pulled the pot off the burner and poured the burned mixture down the sink. She didn't go to the telephone.

I had to grin. He could call until he was blue in the face, but Laura was staying with me.

"Stupid Chris," I said out loud, and the telephone was silent.

"Hey!" said Laura, threatening me with the pot, "just you be quiet, Jenny!"

"But it's true," I said, and Laura grinned.

Now we had to have cocoa out of a box. I could make it by myself. I've been able to do that for a long time. You can't burn it, even if the phone does ring. We sat at the table and Laura handed me a cup. It was red, and so enormous, it was almost a bowl. "This belongs to you now," she said, "no one else will be allowed to use it, just you." She poured in some cocoa for me, and I held the big red bowl of a cup with both hands. My cup. It belonged to me now, forever. It would always sit there, waiting for me until I came. Every Sunday I would drink from my giant red cup. Nobody else could use it. Especially not Chris the Disturber. It would be even better if I could live here, protecting Laura from Chris the Disturber. . . . I wanted to ask her if I could. But then Laura stood up and said we'd have to hurry. Sunday was over and I had to go back. It was late and we were in a rush, so I didn't ask her. Too bad.

We got dressed quick as a flash. There was no time to do each other's buttons. We ran down the stairs and we ran to the train and sat down. We'd hardly caught our breaths before we were back at the Home. That was quick. Much too quick!

"Bye!" said Laura and kissed my cheek briefly, and then she was gone. I hadn't really said good-bye, but next Sunday I'd see her again, there was no doubt about it. I stood around for a while by the front door and looked down the street, but there was no sign of Laura. Instead I saw Andrea coming across the lawn. Why was she coming? Had she been waiting for me? Then I suddenly realized we'd forgotten about her blouse and the book too, the one I'd promised. I wondered if I should try to run away quickly and hide till dinner. Andrea couldn't say anything about it at dinner, we're not allowed to fight then. But I decided to stay where I was. After all, Andrea could fight any time, if not now, then after supper. Better to face her now and get it over with, I decided.

Andrea was already calling, "Where's my blouse? Where's my book, huh?"

"I forgot them," I said. "I'm really sorry, honest." The sorry just came out, just like that.

Of course Andrea exploded. She got furious and called me a lot of mean things, like idiot and liar and thief. Actually, she did have a right to get mad. I should have remembered. A promise is a promise.

I let Andrea go on and said nothing. Maybe her Sunday hadn't been as nice as mine. I was sure she didn't have a giant red cup that belonged to her forever. And she hadn't made up stories about clouds with her Sunday Mommy, or had a picnic in the bathtub. Her Sunday Parents never did things like that with her. But my Sunday Mommy did! She really did!

I stayed calm and left Andrea screaming and went into the dining room. The bell hadn't rung yet, but it was better to be early than late. The table was already set, but there were no kids there yet. Only Donny was hanging around. When he saw me, he smiled and began to drool. I waved at him to say he could sit next to me. Poor thing, he'd had to spend the whole Sunday alone in the Home. He was pretty pale and dirty, especially his hands. We weren't allowed to sit at the table with dirty hands.

I took him to the bathroom. I would wash his hands for him if no one else would, and while we were at it, I might as well wash his face. Donny just stood there entranced. He enjoyed it.

The bell rang. I took Donny by the hand and went back to the dining hall. When Andrea saw me coming in with Donny, she made her eyes cross and grinned rudely. I didn't care. Donny was still little, he needed to be taken care of, and if no one else would do it, I would.

Donny grinned and edged his chair right up to

mine. I pushed him away again, there was no need for him to be that close. But then I cut up his sandwich for him and poured some milk. I think I was able to be so kind to Donny because my own Sunday had been so good.

# Chapter 7

My kindness lasted for a long time, right up to the next Sunday. Whenever something bad happened in school or at the Home, I just thought of Sunday. Then I didn't have to get upset or, at least, not *so* upset.

I explained to Andrea again about forgetting her blouse and forgetting the book; you always have to tell her everything twice or three times. I told her I hadn't forgotten them on purpose just to annoy her, and I promised that I would bring them next Sunday. I also had to promise to bring her Laura's autograph. I thought it was really stupid. Laura was supposed to write "Laura Fielder" on a piece of paper, and I was supposed to give the piece of paper to Andrea.

So then what would she have? A piece of paper

with writing on it. And sooner or later she'd throw it away, anyway. But Andrea said that a piece of paper with an autograph on it would be valuable because Laura was an author. Not that Laura Fielder was famous. No one had heard of her except me, but she was famous enough for an autograph, Andrea said.

I was glad that Laura wasn't famous. I didn't want everyone to know her—just me! Anyway, I think only football players and movie stars are really famous, because you can see them on television. Laura had never been on television. As far as I was concerned, she didn't need to be famous; as far as I was concerned, she just had to be my Sunday Mommy. My Sunday Friend.

And now she was going to pick me up. Any moment. Today was Sunday. It was raining. I'd put on my yellow raincoat with the hood and my yellow boots. I'd inherited them from Andrea because she outgrew them.

As usual I was waiting. As usual the other kids had already left. There was just me there, but I didn't mind. I knew now that Laura would be late. She was always late, it was just the way she was.

Donny wasn't anywhere around. Where could he be hiding? Not that I really like him or anything, but today he could have kept me company while I was waiting. He was probably in the kitchen with Sister Linda, where he likes to be best. Sister Linda is always nice to Donny, she hardly ever gets mad at him. I think that's good. You should try not to get mad at Donny.

Then someone wearing a yellow rain slicker with a hood came hurtling through the door. . . . Laura! She saw me and began to laugh. I began to laugh too. We looked exactly the same, like twins in yellow rain slickers with hoods and yellow boots. How funny! While we were laughing about it, all of a sudden there was Donny hovering nearby, laughing with us. I hadn't heard him coming.

He laughed loudly and tugged at my coat, then he tugged at Laura's, and then suddenly he reached for her hand and held on to it. I thought I must be seeing things. And Laura didn't let go; she held Donny's hand and swung his arm, just like she did with me, and smiled down at Donny and said, "You must be Donny, right?" And Donny grinned up at her and drooled with pleasure.

I was frozen with shock. She was *my* Laura. Nobody else was allowed to hold her like that!

And then Laura ruffled his hair, just like she did mine. That was too much! I grabbed Donny. I held

him really hard and gave him a big shove in the
direction of the kitchen.

Donny stumbled and looked at me with big round
eyes. Then he let go of Laura's hand. He wouldn't
hold her hand again, at least he'd gotten the message.

Laura looked at me in astonishment. I could see
she wasn't pleased about the shove. But I had to stop
him! No one else was allowed to hold on to my Sunday Mommy but me.

I quickly ran out into the street. Then she'd have
to follow me, because she had to go with me, and not
with anyone else. I didn't want her to get any ideas
while she was looking at Donny. It wouldn't be long
before she thought he wasn't so bad. And then she'd
take him with her too.

When Laura caught up with me, I quickly said,
"What are we going to do today?" Now she'd have
to answer me and wouldn't talk about Donny.

But she did talk about him. I knew she would!

"What do you have against Donny?" she asked,
standing near me. Her voice didn't sound angry, it
just sounded surprised, as if she couldn't believe I
had given him a shove.

"I don't have anything against Donny," I said,
looking at the ground. "He just shouldn't hold on to
you, that's all." So now she knew.

Laura didn't say anything for a long time. I didn't look up. She must be going to say something. She'd be mad. I gulped and looked up. . . . Laura was smiling at me. A really long smile. A really loving smile. I couldn't stand to look at it anymore. Then she became very serious. "I don't like shoving, do you understand?"

I nodded quickly, and secretly I made a promise. I wouldn't shove Donny again. Or at least I wouldn't shove him when Laura was around. She took my hand and gave it a squeeze. I squeezed back. She wasn't angry with me. . . .

"Today we're going to do something very different," she said and pulled her hood down and pulled mine down too. "Today I've got to work, the whole day, unfortunately," she said and asked if I would rather stay behind at the Home, because today she wouldn't be able to take care of me. I didn't want to stay behind, no way. I told Laura that she didn't have to take care of me. I'd help her with her work, though I wasn't quite sure how. Laura laughed and said the best way to help would be if I kept quiet, because she had to concentrate, and she asked me if I'd be able to do that for a whole day. I knew that I could, and I'd show her!

I gave Laura a nudge. She should hurry up so we

could get to her house quickly and she could work and I could show her just how quiet I could be. Laura laughed and held me close for a moment and said I was very sweet and that she was very happy to be with me. I thought so too, I was very happy with her.

When we got home, Laura went right to the workshop-kitchen and sat down at her typewriter. I sharpened all her pencils for her, I'm good at that. So now she could do some work. I went into the white room and kept quiet.

Laura had smiled and already had her faraway look. She'd stuck a cigarette in her mouth, put on her glasses, and I shut the kitchen door. Now she was working, writing a story or something.

As I went out I took my giant red cup with me. After all, it did belong to me.

In the white room I first of all sat down on the mattress. The tower of books that I had built last Sunday was still there. Then I remembered I had to give Andrea one of Laura's books. I could pick one out for her now. I began to take down the tower of books and I looked at each one carefully as I did so. But they all had someone else's name on them, none said "Laura Fielder." I couldn't find a single one, she must have lost them all. That would be typical.

I'd just have to ask her where her books were, but not right now. Now she didn't want to be disturbed. She'd see how quiet I could be. Today she wouldn't have to take care of me at all. I'd just ask her later when she took a break.

Would she take a break? She had to. In school when we're working we always have recess. Then we play on the playground and eat our sandwiches.

I knew I could make a recess sandwich for Laura. I'd go into the kitchen and be very quiet.

I carefully opened the door. Laura didn't even notice. She was pounding away on her typewriter and she had her faraway look in spite of her glasses. I realized that last Sunday she hadn't had them on at all, so I'd been able to see her Cuddly-Bunny eyes perfectly. Sometimes she wore them, sometimes she didn't. I guess she needed them when she was working.

I slipped past her quickly and opened the refrigerator. At that she turned around. "Are you hungry?" she asked. I shook my head. She didn't ask any more, but put her cigarette back in her mouth and started pounding away again at the typewriter. I quietly took mayonnaise, ham, and bread out of the refrigerator and I made her a big sandwich. It was just like the one we'd had last Sunday, except this time I made it. The slices of bread were kind of chunky; I'm not very good at cutting bread. But so what, it'd taste good.

I took the sandwich and slipped out of the kitchen again and shut the door quietly behind me. Then I went into the white room and waited until Laura took a break. I'm good at waiting. I sat down on the mattress and looked out of the window. I could make a cloud story, like last time. But there weren't any clouds outside, just rain. I'd make up a rain story instead.

But just then the telephone rang. How loud it sounded! Laura couldn't be disturbed. I bet it was Chris the Disturber. What was I to do? Laura mustn't go to the phone to talk to Chris. Certainly not to him. It would be better if I answered it, but I'd have to be quick. I rushed out and grabbed the receiver from the phone in the hall. The ringing had to stop. It did. Now I'd say something, you always have to say something on the telephone, you can't just stand there holding the receiver. I breathed heavily into it and then I said very quickly and very loudly into the receiver, "Laura can't be disturbed,

Laura is working." And then I put the receiver down.

"What was that?" Laura called from the kitchen. "Wasn't it the phone?"

"No!" I answered back quickly and blushed. Just as well that she couldn't see me. I'd told a lie, but only because I had to.

Laura didn't say anything else, and I went back into the white room with shaky knees. Was it because I'd lied? I'd only wanted to protect Laura so that she could work. The telephone might have disturbed her . . . and so I'd gotten rid of whoever was there. But I didn't feel very happy. I thought I might have been rude on the phone. . . . The main thing was, it was quiet again. Laura's typewriter was tapping, and I was waiting. I'd been waiting quite a long time by now. . . .

Then there was another loud ring. But this time it wasn't the telephone. It was the doorbell, and then someone had opened the front door. I listened. Was it a burglar? But burglars don't ring first, they break in quietly. Should I call Laura, or should I go and see myself?

But then I heard Laura. "Chris!" she cried. Chris! So that was the burglar! How come he was here, how come he'd just opened the door of our apartment?

He shouldn't be here! I went out and there stood Laura, and in front of her stood a giant man who bent down and kissed her on the cheek. I saw him do it. He dared to kiss my Laura. And she seemed to like it; she didn't look at all mad, or disturbed. She even kissed him back, but on his windbreaker, because she couldn't reach his face. He really was very, very tall, this Chris the Disturber, and he had a beard too and glasses, just like Laura's, round and stupid.

He'd have to leave, right now, this minute, he was disturbing us, and anyway . . . anyway, Laura had never kissed *me* on my windbreaker.

"I called," said Chris, "from the phone booth over there, but you have something of a palace guard"—he smiled—"and I wanted to meet her." Then I knew it *had* been Chris earlier on the phone. And it had made absolutely no difference that I had spoken to him. He'd disturbed us anyway.

So he wanted to meet me? Okay, he could, but then he had to leave again, right away. I gulped and went to Laura and stood near her and said very quickly, "Laura has to work, she can't be disturbed." And as I said it I looked very sternly at Chris so that he would get the point. It was my Sunday and she was my Laura.

"I've heard that once today already," said Chris. He took off his windbreaker and got us all wet with raindrops. Then he took my hand, shook it, and said, "How do you do. So you're the palace guard, are you?"

"Yes, that's who she is," said Laura, putting her arm round me and squeezing me tight. "And you are disturbing me." But she said it as if she didn't mean it. I didn't believe her, and Chris didn't believe her, either.

"Just go back to work," he said, pushing Laura gently into the kitchen. "We'll manage on our own." And he marched into the white room and plunked down on the mattress. "Come on," he said to me, "so I don't disturb Laura." She had gone back to her workshop-kitchen and shut the door and the typewriter was clattering away once more.

I went over and sat down next to Chris. Not too close. He was fidgeting around on the mattress with his long legs, but at least he had taken his shoes off. He was wearing socks that didn't match, a blue striped one and a red one. It looked funny. Didn't he know that socks should match?

Chris grinned at me, but I didn't grin back, even though his grin looked really nice and the corners of his mouth disappeared into his beard.

And then he started to ask questions. What it was like in the Home and at school and whether I had friends and . . . and . . .

I answered. You have to answer questions, it's polite, and anyway, I thought that once he knew everything about me and had gotten to know me, he'd go away again!

Wishful thinking! He didn't go, he stayed. He'd made himself comfortable on the mattress and talked about himself. That he was a teacher and where he lived and that he liked kids, but not all of them, and then he talked about Laura. About her work, and about what it's like when you write a book, and how it works, and he talked about the publisher, that was someone who would publish her books, and then they would get printed, and he explained exactly how that worked. He talked to me as if I were a grown-up. Other grown-ups never talked to me like that, only Laura. And then Chris said that if I wanted, he would take me to a publisher one day to see how books were made. I quickly asked him if publishers were open on Sundays, because I was only allowed out on Sundays. They were all closed on Sundays, Chris said, but he'd take me one day during the week if I wanted. He'd make sure it was all right with the Home, he said.

By this time I decided that Chris was all right. Actually, he was really nice. I bet he was even a good teacher if he was the way he was with me with his class. Besides, he said such great things about Laura and me. He said how proud he was of her, because she wrote wonderful children's books, and he told me how much she'd changed since I'd been coming. He said that she had really "blossomed," and that he was even a little bit jealous, because she hadn't "blossomed" like that because of him for a long time.

I realized he liked Laura very much and that he was sad he had to share her. I could understand that. I don't like sharing, either. But I told him I only had Laura on Sundays, he could have her to himself the whole week.

Then Chris gave me a long look through his stupid round glasses and said, "I think that's going to change. If I know Laura . . ." He stopped and reached out and took a bite of the sandwich. Laura's sandwich! Now he was gulping it down! And in between mouthfuls he said, "Laura thinks Sundays with you are much too short." I didn't hear right, I was watching Laura's sandwich disappear into his mouth. Little pieces of ham were left clinging to his beard.

Suddenly Laura stood in the doorway. She rubbed her eyes under her glasses and asked, "What are you two up to?"

"He ate your sandwich!" I said, pointing at Chris. And then I had to laugh. He made a face as if he'd just been scolded.

Laura stopped rubbing her eyes. With a leap she jumped over to me and grabbed me and said, "You made that for me?" I nodded.

"Hand it over!" exclaimed Laura to Chris. "It's mine!" And she made a grab for the piece that Chris still had in his hand.

"You're going to get spoiled, I'd like to have food as good as this once in a while!" he cried and held the sandwich up high. And then the two of them started fooling around like kids. They tickled each other and squealed and screeched, and I just sat there grinning at them. It was worse than in the school playground. Then suddenly there I was in the middle of their fight. There was no time to wonder about it. I had to protect myself because they were both so good at tickling.

"Stop!" cried Laura in the end. She looked like a bird with half its feathers plucked out.

"Stop!" cried Chris too. He didn't look much better, especially around his beard.

"As punishment let's all go out to supper," he said, combing his beard with his fingers. "I'll be the one who has to pay."

"I'll believe that when I see it!" said Laura and turned to me. "Would you like to go?" Of course I'd like to. I always like eating out.

"But what about your work?" I asked. She still had to work.

"Finished," said Laura. She went to the kitchen and came back with a large manila envelope. "Stamped and addressed, ready to be mailed, and you can put it in the mailbox. That'll bring me luck."

I took the envelope and held it tight. I couldn't lose it. There was Laura's work inside it. What kind of work? A story, she'd said, a children's story. Maybe she would tell it to me one day. I don't like reading to myself, being told a story is quicker.

We put our coats on and then I remembered just in time about Andrea's blouse, Andrea's book, and the piece of paper with Laura's autograph. This time I really would not forget. Laura said she'd already gotten everything ready, she was going to give me a copy of the book anyway and she'd just put in one more for Andrea, and she'd quickly write an autograph. I watched her write her name on a piece of paper. Laura Fielder. It looked very nice. I might even keep the piece of paper for myself.

And then off we went. The three of us. Chris had a car, and he was going to drive us to a restaurant. I knew one on the corner opposite the Home. I'd never been in it. Only the big kids go there sometimes after school and they hang out there on Sundays too.

Chris's car wasn't the most beautiful: it was very old and rattled so much while it drove that you could hardly hear yourself speak.

In front of the restaurant was a mailbox into which I dropped the fat manila envelope. Chris and Laura watched. Chris held the flap open for me and Laura spat three times after it, "pth—pth—pth!" to bring even more luck.

Then we went into the restaurant. I was hoping a couple of the older kids would be there so they would see—me and my Sunday Mommy and Chris. He wasn't disturbing us anymore, in fact, he was getting along very well with us. Laura and I were like little twin dwarves beside him. It was funny. And there *were* some kids from the Home in the restaurant. When they saw me, they stared and made faces. So I stuck out my tongue at them. So there!

We ordered hot chocolate and I remembered I

hadn't used my giant red cup today. It wouldn't run away. And Chris wouldn't drink out of it. I thought I could ask him to promise not to. I picked our desserts, Laura said I could. I picked chocolate cake. And then I discovered it was Laura's favorite cake too. We didn't ask Chris what his was, he'd just have to eat what he paid for.

We chomped away, and I sat very close to Laura and she smiled at me and she chattered to Chris about her work and he chattered about school, and I looked across at the other kids to make sure they could see me sitting there with the two of them. The plastic shopping bag with Andrea's blouse, the two books, and the piece of paper with Laura's autograph was clamped firmly between my knees so I wouldn't forget it.

We sat there for a long time. Chris ordered another piece of chocolate cake. I could just go on eating chocolate cake and sitting next to Laura forever.

But then she looked at the time, and Sunday was over once more. I had to go back to the Home because that's where I lived and you always have to go back to where you live. Laura kissed me good-bye on the cheek. Chris didn't kiss me, thank goodness, his beard would have been scratchy. He shook my hand, gave a little bow, and said he was most grateful for such a delightful afternoon and hoped he would have the pleasure of meeting me again soon. He was really funny. Was he like that with his class? I wondered. If he was, they were really lucky. . . .

Laura and Chris got back into his old rattletrap car and drove off. Laura waved at me from the window for a long time . . . then she was gone, they were both gone.

When I went into the Home, I bumped right into Andrea. I always meet her first. But this time I had a clear conscience. I handed her the plastic shopping bag and she unpacked it right away. She's so nosy.

She tucked the blouse under one arm and shoved the piece of paper into her pants pocket without even looking at it, but she did start leafing through the books. Two books? I remembered that one of them was actually for me. Laura had given it to me. It was still mine, whether I read it or not. Luckily Andrea realized this, otherwise we'd have had another fight. With a stupid grin on her face, she handed me one of the books. It was opened up, and on the first page was written, "For my Sunday's Child, with love from Laura." She had written that for me. I wished Andrea hadn't seen it.

In her book there was only "For Andrea, from Laura Fielder." That wasn't as nice as what was in mine, but even so, I think she was pleased. She didn't make any stupid comment, she just sat down in the hall and began to read. She can do that for hours and hours.

I went up to our room, to Cuddly-Bunny. I read him what Laura had written so that he would be pleased too. "For my Sunday's Child, with love from Laura." And I decided that one day soon I would read the whole book from beginning to end because that would make Laura happy.

# Chapter 8

I almost couldn't wait until the end of that week. I kept wondering what we would do on Sunday and whether Chris would visit us again. It was okay with me, as long as he didn't stay too long. . . . I half expected him to come and take me to the publishers, but he didn't come.

On Monday I had a brilliant idea. I would bake a cake as a surprise for Laura. A chocolate cake like the one we'd eaten in the restaurant, only even nicer. The chocolate cakes we have here, when someone has a birthday, are actually better than the ones in the restaurant because they have a number made out of little sugar balls on top, a six or a nine or an eleven or whatever, depending on how old you are. I thought of writing "Laura" on top in little sugar balls; it would look very pretty.

I asked Sister Linda whether I could make a cake for Laura. She thought about it and then said I could as a special treat. She understood that I wanted to please my Sunday Mommy, since Laura hadn't been my Sunday Mommy for very long. But what would please my Sunday Mommy best of all, she said, would be if I were a good little girl. But it was obvious I was one already. All she had to do was ask Laura.

I wanted to start baking right away, but Sister Linda said I should wait until Saturday, because then the cake would be fresh. A cake baked on Monday would be hard as a rock by Sunday; it wouldn't taste good at all. I saw her point. So I waited until Saturday, but the time passed so slowly. I didn't read any of Laura's book. Only what she had written in it; I looked at that every evening and read it out loud to Cuddly-Bunny. He knew it all by heart now, and so did I. I kept the book under my pillow and slept on it.

To make the week pass more quickly, I played with Donny quite a lot. Donny liked playing really stupid games, baby games like "Eeny-meeny-miny-mo, catch a tiger by his toe, if he hollers, let him go, eeny-meeny-miny-mo!"

I also played Lego with him, but he's even less

good at that. I'm great at it. I can even make a car with a trailer and a bulldozer. Donny thought that was fantastic. If it were up to him, I'd always be building him bulldozers. Of course I didn't have that much time. I told him that I would build him one bulldozer every day, and in return he had to promise not to come into the hall on Sunday and hold on to Laura because Laura was mine. I couldn't help it if he didn't have anyone.

So Donny promised, drooling away and grinning, but I wasn't sure if he really understood. So what? A promise is a promise. I even told him he could help me make the chocolate cake.

Andrea was amazed that I was spending so much time with Donny. She started muttering something about "lovebirds" again, but only quietly. She was really nice to me, in fact, because I had brought her the book and the autograph. So she left me in peace and even swapped beds with me once. But even so, it was a long wait till Sunday.

Sometimes days just flash past. I get up, and suddenly it's already evening again and I'm back in bed. And then there are other days that creep past. They take forever. This week was like that. A creeping week.

Saturday was better. I was allowed to bake the

cake with Sister Linda and Donny. Donny got in the way a lot, but I'd promised him he could help. I let him eat some of the cake decorations that he had managed to ruin. I didn't want them on my beautiful cake. Then I quickly made a bulldozer for him, just to make sure he wouldn't come to the hall on Sunday and hold on to Laura.

Then, at last, Sunday arrived.

I sat in the hall and waited, as usual. I had the sponge cake on my lap. Sister Linda had packed it up carefully in aluminum foil. It looked pretty. I held on to the cake tightly and felt very happy about seeing Laura and about Sunday. When I thought of what it used to be like on Sundays, I couldn't believe I ever stood it. Sundays used to be long and thin, and all I ever did was wait for them to be over. Now my Sundays were round and fat, like a coat with its pockets full and something hidden in every pocket— something funny or nice or just a surprise.

Donny wasn't in the hall. He was being so good. Unfortunately, Laura wasn't in the hall either. She was late again. What a dope she was. I had something special for her today. She'd be really surprised. I'd jump up to meet her and hug her around her neck, I'd never dared do that before. Then I'd give her the cake, right away, and she'd be so pleased and we'd take it home together and eat it on the mattress, and I'd drink chocolate milk from my giant cup. That would be better, real cocoa never works for us. And if Chris came, he could have a piece of cake too, but first I'd tell him off for not taking me to the publishers. I didn't really want to see the publishers that much, but I did want to get taken out.

By then it was already nine-thirty. Laura still hadn't come. She'd never been as late as this. She must be coming any minute now, I thought.

Then there was Sister Linda coming down the stairs. I lifted up the cake and grinned at her. We'd made it together. But Sister Linda didn't smile back, she stopped still and said, "Oh, my goodness me!" She sounded really shocked.

And then I realized it didn't have anything to do with the cake, it was something else. Something horrible . . .

Sister Linda came and sat down beside me and said, "I'm so very sorry dear, but Miss Fielder isn't coming because . . ." I put my hands over my ears, and at that the sponge cake fell on the floor. *"Miss Fielder isn't coming."* Laura wasn't coming. She wasn't coming to take me out!

Sister Linda took my hands away from my ears

and said, "Now let me explain . . ." But I tore myself away, I didn't want to hear, and I ran upstairs to our room. Sister Linda ran after me, but I slammed the door in her face. Really hard. I didn't want to hear and I didn't want to see her. If Laura wasn't coming, I didn't want to see anybody.

Sister Linda didn't come into the room. I threw myself on my bed and clutched Cuddly-Bunny. Laura wasn't coming at all this Sunday. She was leaving me here by myself. Why? Didn't she want me anymore? But I'd made a chocolate cake for her. By next Sunday it would be stale. . . . And who knows whether she'd come next Sunday anyway, who knows whether she'd ever come again? And anyway, if she wasn't coming today, she didn't have to bother to come anymore. . . . Now I knew the truth, now I knew it all. She wouldn't come anymore. She'd realized she liked Chris more than me, that she'd rather be alone with him. It was all Chris's fault, I'd been right the first time. Damn Chris. I thumped Cuddly-Bunny down on the bed and screamed, "Damn Chris," and tore at Cuddly-Bunny's ear. He couldn't help it, but Chris could; it was his fault. It was Laura's fault too because she hadn't picked me up. I wanted to go to Laura. This very minute.

I wanted her to come and get me. This very minute! I couldn't stay here in the Home all Sunday. I'd refuse!

I called out really loudly, "Laura!" and threw Cuddly-Bunny across the room.

Suddenly Sister Linda was in the room. Why had she come? She must have been listening. She said, "Now don't get so worked up. You're behaving as though you hate the Home."

I was not getting worked up. And I did hate the Home. So there!

Sister Linda came and sat down and tried to take my hand. That was the last straw, I refused to have my hand held. I only let Laura do that, I only wanted Laura to hold my hand. . . . So I hit Sister Linda. I wasn't sorry at all. And I yelled, "Go away, go away, go away!" And when she didn't go away, I hit her again, so hard in the stomach that it hurt. Sister Linda went white and grabbed her stomach, but she said nothing, she stood up . . . and when I saw her standing there, so tall, so completely different from Laura, I wanted to do something to make her explode, I wanted to make the whole orphanage explode . . . and I just screamed as loud as I could, "Damn it, go away!"

She did go then, she left the door open. I didn't care. I screamed. . . .

Then Sister Linda was back in the room. Only it wasn't Sister Linda, it was Sister Frances. I didn't care about that, either. I screamed. . . .

I had to scream, otherwise I would have burst. I screamed for a long time, then suddenly Sister Frances said, "Now that's enough!" She took my hand, pulled me up from the bed, and slapped me on both cheeks. Not hard, but still, she'd never slapped me on the cheek before. I was so surprised, I shut my mouth. "There!" said Sister Frances, then she let go of me, and I just slid to the floor like a sack of potatoes and stayed there.

My legs were suddenly so tired. My head was so tired. I slumped on the floor in front of Sister Frances and felt sick. I wanted her to go. I wanted to cuddle up to Cuddly-Bunny and crawl into bed and never, never get up again.

"Can I talk to you now?" asked Sister Frances. I thought to myself, If she starts on about a nice cup of tea, I'll scream again and keep screaming till I have no voice left. But she didn't say anything about tea. She came and sat on my bed and said again, "I want to talk to you."

Go on, then. I wouldn't listen. I'd never listen to anyone again. They only told lies. I didn't make a sound, I just stayed on the floor and hoped she'd hurry up and then go away.

She began very gently, but very loudly. I wanted to crawl under the bed, but I couldn't. Her fat legs were in the way. How could anyone have such fat legs? Laura's were much thinner, almost like mine. Now I'd never see Laura's thin legs again, I knew that. I wanted to bite Sister Frances's legs. I wanted to bite myself.

Cuddly-Bunny must be broken—my only friend, Cuddly-Bunny. The only one who listened to me. There he lay in front of the window, one ear half torn off. I had done that. Suddenly my face was full of water, it streamed out of my eyes and out of my nose. I let it.

Sister Frances started talking. About me. "We have the impression," she said, "that your contact with Miss Fielder is very close."

Contact! That sounded like an electric plug. We loved each other! I loved her! She didn't love me. Otherwise she wouldn't have left me here by myself. If I was her, I'd never have left me here by myself on a Sunday.

Sister Frances went on talking, she didn't even

notice that I was sobbing. "We think that's very nice," she said, ruffling my hair a little as she said it. I wrenched my head away, I didn't want her touching it. Not her or anybody else, either.

"We do want the best for our children," she said.

I was not her child, I was a Sunday's Child, Laura's Sunday Child.

"We recently had a conversation with Miss Fielder and her friend," said Sister Frances. I listened. A conversation? Had Laura been here, then, and not come to see me?

"I invited them here," continued Sister Frances. "I felt it was necessary to have a discussion about you."

Laura had been here! Chris too! He'd come too, and they had all talked about me, and I hadn't been allowed to be there. That was mean. I wouldn't have done that. I would have come to see me. She was a traitor. I stuck my head between my knees and clenched my fists, to stop myself from screaming again. I was still crying as it was.

"I'm now going to tell you something I hadn't intended to tell you," said Sister Frances, "at least not for the time being." Why did she say that? She could keep it to herself anyway, it was all the same to me.

"I want you to listen to me," she continued, and suddenly she picked me up off the floor, and before I could struggle and object, she'd put me on her lap. I think the last time I had sat there was when I was a baby. My face was right up close to hers, and her face had lots of creases and wrinkles and didn't look at all like Laura's, and I buried my head in her shoulder so that I wouldn't see it. Sister Frances's face. If I didn't look at it, and just felt what it was like sitting on her lap, I could almost imagine it was Laura's lap. Even though hers wasn't nearly as big.

"Now listen," said Sister Frances, speaking into my hair right next to my ear. "Listen. We've been considering with Miss Fielder and her friend whether an adoption might be possible."

It tickled when she talked into my ear like that. She had murmured something . . . what had she said? I didn't know. My head was so tired . . . she rocked me back and forth like a baby. I'd like to be a baby . . . I'd like to be Laura's baby. . . . I said quietly into Sister Frances's shoulder, "Why didn't she come and pick me up?"

"Because we thought it would be better if Miss Fielder spent today going through the question of adoption with her friend. We must all become some-what objective at this point," answered Sister

Frances, stroking my hair. The question of adoption . . . what did that mean, what did she have to go through? The question of adoption. Adoption . . . I sat up. Adoption. I knew about that. That was something really incredible. Some of the children in the Home had gotten parents who they could keep forever. Those children had never come back to the Home except every once in a while for a visit. The children had been adopted.

I whispered softly, "Adopted."

"Yes," said Sister Frances, "adopted. You know what that means?" I knew. It was something ultra-super-fantastic. You had parents forever!

"Well," said Sister Frances, and she said that to my face because now I was looking at her, "Miss Fielder would very much like to adopt you." She kept on talking, but I couldn't listen anymore, I just couldn't. My stomach had started to tingle.

Laura wanted to adopt me. She wanted me to be her child all the time, not just on Sundays. She wanted . . . I think my face must have looked very odd, because Sister Frances suddenly began to talk very fast. She said, "I must also warn you not to set your heart on it. Nothing has been finalized yet. In Miss Fielder's case, it will certainly be very difficult. Listen to me, it may be impossible. Are you listening? It might be necessary for her and her friend to get married, so that you would have regular parents, and Miss Fielder and her friend must make a decision about that first, do you understand? And even if they do get married, it will take time. I don't want to rouse any false hopes, perhaps nothing will come of it, and then what?" She shook me, and I wobbled in her hands, on her lap, like a rubber doll.

Of course I had been listening. I was going to be adopted. Laura was going to adopt me. We'd get Chris too, but that didn't matter. Laura would be my real mother. For always.

I think I was still crying. But differently. Sister Frances pulled me closer to her and said, "Oh, my Jenny, my dear, I do so hope it works out for you. But suppose it doesn't? We must think of that. Oh, my dear."

Suddenly it was all very strange. Sister Frances's voice sounded as if it were on the verge of tears. That couldn't be. She shouldn't cry. Of course it would work out. If Laura wanted it to and I wanted it to and Chris helped also, then of course it would work out. I was sure of it. There was nothing to cry about. It was just a question of waiting. Sister Frances had said that herself. Waiting quite a while, perhaps. But then, I could wait, I was good at waiting. I really didn't mind that.

Anyway, I was a Sunday's Child, after all. And children born on a Sunday are lucky. Of course they are.

# Chapter 9

Best of all, I would have liked to have just sat down and waited for my luck to come along. All day Monday. And all day Tuesday and Wednesday for as long as it took till Laura came to pick me up. So that I could stay with her forever.

But she didn't come and pick me up and I couldn't just sit and wait. I had to go to school, of course. That was awful. You always have to go to school. Except when you're sick, then you don't have to.

I think I *was* a little sick from waiting. I even told Sister Frances. I felt so funny, so wobbly . . . I could tell Sister Frances that now because she understood me, I was sure she did. She was always looking at me in such a funny way, so differently from before. I knew why. We had a secret. But I did have to go to school. Sister Frances said that the time would go by quickest if I did what I always did. And that I shouldn't dwell on it too much. Otherwise I might "come back down to earth with a bump." I have no idea what she really meant. But she had stroked my hair as she said it. I hadn't told Andrea or anyone else about the adoption. I'd have to be sure it would happen first, sure.

But as soon as it did I'd tell her. Or maybe, even better, I'd just pack Cuddly-Bunny and all my things and when Andrea asked where I was going, I'd say really casually, "Oh, I'm going to be adopted, if you must know. Bye." She'd be amazed! And jealous.

Whenever I thought about it, I got really warm, in my stomach and in my head. To be adopted was the best thing of all.

I think Sister Linda knew something about it too. At night, when we went to bed, she'd give me two good night kisses. That was nice because secretly I'd imagine it was Laura kissing me, although Laura's kisses weren't as wet.

I think Sister Linda was going to miss me a lot because she'd started paying a lot of attention to me.

She acted as if I'd soon be gone. Whenever she could catch me, she would touch me. I let myself be caught all the time because the touching was like the kissing. I'd shut my eyes and imagine Laura. My Sunday Mommy. No, my *real* mommy.

I wondered what she was doing now. Was she rearranging the apartment? She only had one bed. She'd have to buy another one for me and a bed was probably expensive. Laura had so little money. If she couldn't buy a bed, I wouldn't be allowed to move in with her because the people in the Home wanted me to be well taken care of. But Chris had money. He had a real job and a car. And in the restaurant he'd bought us both dinner and never complained. He'd have to give Laura money for a bed. Married people have to share their money like that. And Chris would have to marry us. Well, Laura really, but he'd get me too. This was going to be expensive for Chris. I only hoped we had enough money. I'd have liked to have asked him, but I didn't know where he lived. Just somewhere around the corner from Laura.

Now, that was really stupid. These people were going to be my parents and I didn't even know where I could reach my father. I could have asked

Sister Frances, I suppose, but I didn't dare. She looked as if she didn't want to be asked anything more.

I had a strange time until Saturday. I felt as if my head had grown because I had to think about so many things. Andrea wondered why I'd been so quiet. She thought I was getting a cold. At least then she left me alone, she didn't want to catch it. . . . If only she knew. . . .

On Saturday I couldn't stand it anymore or my head would have burst. I told Donny everything. He didn't really understand any of it. I built him three bulldozers and while I was doing that I told him everything. Donny beamed and nodded all the time and didn't dribble at all. He was so happy about the bulldozers. He laughed out loud and his cheeks got pink. You could really see the difference. Rosy cheeks looked good with his straw-colored hair. He almost looked handsome.

I promised him that if I was adopted, he could come and visit us. Then I could show him the apartment. And if he was very good, we would take him with us on a trip. But he would have to be extra-specially good for that, and always hold Chris's hand. He'd have to promise that. Laura's hand belonged to me because she was my mother. Donny nodded again and croaked, "Chris." Only it sounded more like "Kiss." I had to laugh. Donny still had a lot to learn. But maybe he was learning. He was still only little.

I wasn't going to let Andrea visit us. At least, not yet. She always giggled and acted stupid around grown-ups and made dumb remarks to me. She could come and see us later . . . maybe.

I just couldn't live normally because I had to wait. I didn't really belong in the Home, and I didn't really belong to Laura yet, either. I was somewhere in between. Funny. I wished I could just sleep through it all, then wake up and be adopted.

Sister Frances was calling. Donny dropped his bulldozer and I dropped Donny's hand. I'd been holding it in mine and hadn't even noticed. I raced off. Sister Frances had called in such a strangled voice. She didn't usually call like that. She must have something important to tell me. I knew what it was. . . . I ran. Three steps at a time. I flew. Four steps at a time . . . and I landed on my hands and knees on the floor. Smack in front of Sister Frances. I could tell by the fat legs. But there were other legs as well. Long thin ones . . . and even thinner ones. I recognized them. I knew them well. Laura had come. And Chris too. They'd come to pick me up. Now, this minute. Or had they?

Then someone laughed out loud. It was Chris. "Prostrate in front of her parents! That really isn't necessary!" He laughed. I looked up, straight into the laughing face of Sister Frances.

Laura wasn't laughing. She just stood there, looking at me. Her glasses were misting up, I could see that. I was still sitting on the floor as if I'd fallen on my head instead of on my knees. "Parents," Chris had said. They were my parents and I'd fallen down the stairs in front of them. How stupid can you get?

There was a buzzing in my head and I pulled myself together and ran back up the stairs. Away. To Donny. I grabbed hold of him. Donny didn't have the slightest idea what was happening to him. His eyes opened wide and he began to drool. I took hold of his hand firmly and pulled him down the stairs. He stumbled after me and when we got to the bottom, I said, and by then I almost had no breath left, "Can Donny come and visit us?" and I held tightly on to him.

Then they all started to laugh at once. Chris laughed the loudest, and Sister Frances cackled and wiped her eyes. Donny and I just stood there. I didn't understand myself. I hadn't wanted to say that. I had wanted to ask about something . . . to find out what they had to tell me. Suddenly Laura was next to me. She laughed and hugged me tight. She squeezed me close. And then I realized how homesick I'd been the whole week long. For Laura. I had been almost sick . . . but now she was here. Now I could see her and hear her and feel her. Now I could ask her what I wanted to ask. "Am I adopted now?"

"Not yet," said Laura and stopped laughing, but she didn't let go of me. "But soon, as quickly as we can," she said, holding me tight. "That's a promise. But first of all you'll stay with me on trial."

"On trial," I said, and Laura nodded.

"Promise," I said, and Laura nodded again.

"A trial daughter," Chris said with a smile, and Sister Frances cleared her throat.

There wasn't a buzzing in my head anymore. My head was very clear. My head was very light.

"Trial father," I murmured and groped for Laura's hand.

"A trial time," said Sister Frances and cleared her throat again.

"A trial marriage," I said and gave a grin. At Chris.

"A trial spanking." He grinned back.

"Trial mommy?" I asked and gave Laura's hand a squeeze.

She shook her head and squeezed back. It almost hurt, but it felt good because I knew how it was meant.

"Daughter," she said. She said it very quietly. But I had heard. I heard.

"Now, how about a nice cup of tea?" suggested Sister Frances, and marched off. "There's a lot to discuss."

I had to burst out laughing. It had happened again. Sister Frances and her tea!

"Trial tea!" I roared and squealed. "Trial discussion. In the trial room. Trial cookies!"

"I think you're going bananas!" said Chris, taking Donny by the hand.

"Trial bananas!" I shrieked and was hardly able to get the words out because laughter was rumbling around inside my stomach.

Donny laughed too. And how! He hopped around, holding Chris's hand, and crowed and squeaked. Poor Donny . . . he didn't understand. But how happy he was. . . . "Trial brother!" I laughed and gave him a push. At that Donny clung tightly to me and said, very loudly and very clearly, "I am your Sunday Brother!"

I stopped laughing. Everyone stopped laughing. Donny had said his first whole sentence! People were making a big fuss about him and ignoring me, but for once I didn't even mind.

# About the Author

Gudrun Mebs is the award-winning author of six books for young readers. *Sunday's Child* has been published in fourteen countries.

It received the coveted German Children's Book Prize, West Germany's equivalent of the Newbery Medal. Ms. Mebs also works as a stage and television actress and has toured the world in both adult and children's theater productions.

| DATE DUE | | | |
|---|---|---|---|
| 17 | | | |
| APR 28 '90 | | | |
| APR 17 '90 | | | |
| 18 | | | |
| APR 24 '90 | | | |
| 13 | | | |
| MAY 21 '90 | | | |
| 17 | | | |
| OCT - 6 '98 | | | |
| 25 | | | |
| NOV 24 | | | |

Meb     Mebs, Gudrun

Sunday's child

PARK ORCHARD ELEM
Kent, Washington

 Bound to Stay Bound Books, Inc.